To: Linda

DIE CUT

Crafty Sleuth

NELLE HERAN & C.K. EASTLAND

Thank you
for being a healing
and supportive force of
nature!! I love you & Jim!
C.K. Eastland

Die Cut

Cover art: Covers in Color, coversincolor.com
Edited by: Sunwalker Press; Meg DesCamp

ISBN: 978-1-947033-42-9

First edition
March 2022

Contact information:
nelle@nelleheran.com
ck@ckeastland.com

DIE CUT

Crafty Sleuth

NELLE HERAN &
C.K. EASTLAND

CHAPTER ONE

I had three goals for my visit to the Paper and Fiber Arts Crafting Expo, and I was already failing at priority number one: keeping my friend Ava from buying more craft supplies than any ten people could use.

In their entire lifetimes.

We were only four booths inside the doors of the exhibit hall —a big, high-ceilinged barracks of a place—and I was already weighed down with bags full of Ava's impulse buys. On the other hand, my own oversized reusable shopping bag was still empty.

"Ava, do you have a plan for all these supplies?"

Ava didn't look up from sorting through paper packs. "Not yet. But you never know when an idea might strike."

Calling Ava my friend wasn't precisely correct. She was more a legacy: She'd been a critical care nurse who'd gotten my grandfather through his triple bypass surgery and recovery. She'd relocated to Portland with her family after her husband retired, but when he passed and her adult daughter moved out of state, Pops asked me to look out for her. *"She'll be alone in a new place, Tashie. She'll need a friend."*

My bestie, PJ, claimed Ava didn't need a friend so much as an intervention, but he loved Pops as much as I did and both of us would do anything for him.

So I'd reached out, and Ava had joined my circle of crafting friends about two years ago. She'd promptly remodeled her empty nest—including adding a state-of-the-art craft room—even though at that point, she'd never crafted a thing in her life. Since then, she'd filled the room to bursting with supplies and started dozens of projects, only to abandon them when they didn't match up to her vision. But her belief that the next one would be *The One* never faded.

"You know, Tash," she said, poking at chipboard embellishments, "sometimes I don't think you're serious about crafting at all."

I blinked at her—or rather, at the pilled back of her pink cardigan, which was all I could see since she'd dived headfirst into a bin of washi tape.

Me? Not serious? Yes, all my crafts were hobbies, since my job as a technical marketing manager was what paid the bills. But my friends called me the Craft Whisperer. They teased me constantly about my ability to produce a project suited to almost any occasion on demand.

"What makes you say that?"

She stood up and jerked her chin at me. "Well, just look at you. You haven't bought a single thing, and we've already been here for twenty minutes."

"I like to walk the whole show before I make any purchases."

"But somebody else could grab the treasures first. You've got to strike early." She pounded one fist into the opposite palm. "Beat the crowds."

"Beat the crowds, huh?" I peered around the vast, cement-floored hall. For some reason, the place was practically empty. Heck, there were more security personnel roaming the aisles than customers. Granted, it was a sunny day in early June—unusual in Portland, where we expected clouds and drizzle at least until the end of the month—so folks might be out soaking up a little bonus vitamin D. But this show had always been packed before.

Ava patted me on the shoulder. "I know you mean well, Tash, and your little projects generally look lovely, of course, but you need to stop limiting yourself. Think bigger. Think *more.*" She pointed to a display of Swarovski crystals. "More bling! More colors! More flair!"

Flair? Really?

"But don't you think you ought to pace yourself? You're three hundred dollars down, and we've still got an acre of booths to visit."

Her mouth twisted in disdain. "Thanks to Charles's hefty life insurance policy, three hundred dollars is nothing. Let me tell you, the best thing that man ever did for me was die." Her gaze slid past me and her eyes lit up. "Oooh, Tash, look. *Ribbons!*" Her topknot of graying locs bounced on her head as she beelined to the neighboring booth. I sighed and followed in time to have her stack ten spools of ribbon in my hands. I fumbled them, but smooshed them against my stomach in a last-minute save before they could tumble to the ground.

Ava *tsk*ed. "Careful, there, Tash. These cement floors are always grimy. If you drop something, it could get dirty." She peered around as the vendor ran her credit card. "Where's your little friend, anyway? What's his name? Pretty? Party? Putty?"

I hid a wince. "Purdy. PJ Purdy." PJ just rolls his eyes whenever Ava gets his name wrong since she seems to do it just to get a rise out of us, but he'd have taken *strong* exception to being called *little.* Was he smaller than me? Yes, but then so many people were. He always insists that five-nine is absolutely average for a man, declaring, "I'm not *small.* I'm *medium.*" Besides, what PJ lacks in size, he makes up in attitude.

"Purdy, then. I thought he was supposed to meet you here with a hand truck." Ava thrust a pair of sleeved scissors at me without looking to see if I'd grabbed it before she let go. "It's not very thoughtful of him, making you carry all this stuff around."

"I'm sure he's got a good reason." And I was starting to get worried. PJ was many things, but *late* wasn't one of them. "He's bound to be here—"

"Ooh, look, Tash. *Alcohol inks!*"

And she was off again in a patter of pink orthopedic sneakers, leaving me to collect her bag of ribbons. At this rate, I'd be trailing her all day and never accomplish my second goal —to learn at least two new techniques I could use as fresh content for the classes I taught at local craft stores.

I scanned the nearby exhibits while Ava cooed over the ink display. All my favorite vendors had booths here—Graphic 45, Bo Bunny, Tim Holtz, Copic—as well as a lot of independent suppliers. I gazed yearningly at the Blue Moon Scrapbooking booth. Maybe if I steered Ava in that direction...

"Did you see this?" Ava tugged on my elbow, and I nearly dropped all her bags. To be safe, I set them on the floor at our feet. "When you buy the whole set, they *give* you this neat special edition storage and carrying case. For free!" It was more likely that the cost of the completely unremarkable toolbox was buried in the set's pricing structure, but I doubted Ava would believe me.

After all, I wasn't *serious* about crafting.

I sighed. That ridiculous ink holder did *not* look light—it was probably made from particle board, for Pete's sake—and I had few illusions about who would be carrying it around for the rest of the day. Or until PJ got here with the hand cart, at any rate.

As Ava zeroed in on a mini paper craft sewing machine in neon green—*no, please no*—I spotted a booth beyond the Blue Moon exhibit, tucked in the corner behind a giant fiber arts display. From what little I could make out through an enormous macrame sunburst, their inventory looked interesting. I'm a big believer in supporting local businesses whenever I can—and when I can keep Ava from getting distracted by the next shiny object.

I glanced at her. Yup, she was adding that hideous sewing machine to her purchases. Could I sneak away to check out that tempting display?

I *hmmmph*ed, glancing down at my outfit, and heard PJ's voice in my head: "LaTashia Danielle Fredericka Van Buren, you are a six foot tall, plus-sized, tawny-skinned *goddess,* and you're wearing a navy crinoline dress decorated with *huge* white scissors, and a cocktail hat with *feathers.* You are incapable of *sneaking* anywhere."

Of course, since I'd completed my look today with my navy and white platform Chuck Taylor's, I was more like six foot three—not counting the feathers—but I'd learned to embrace my height a long time ago. Besides, I'd purposely dressed to attract attention today since my third priority was to drum up interest in the class I was teaching tomorrow at Central Paper and Supply.

Nevertheless, Ava was so intent on buying the totally unnecessary sewing machine that she didn't spot me sidling away, and I escaped undetected, at least by her. The corner booth—Dianne's DooDads—was a mixed-media dream, all about ornamentation. It was laid out like a candy store—tilted wide-mouthed jars full of miscellaneous bits and bobs, sold by the ounce and arranged by color. Little scoops were attached to each jar with bejeweled chains so patrons could serve themselves. More elaborate embellishments hung in small bags above the jars. A woman in a *Dianne's DooDads* apron was listlessly transferring the by-the-ounce tchotchkes into mini mason jars and slotting them into wooden bins in strict color spectrum sets. Since her name tag read *Dianne,* I figured she must be the owner. She perked up when I leaned over the table to pick up an apothecary bottle full of mixed red crystals and buttons.

"Wow." Her eyes widened as she took in my dress. "Your outfit is fabulous!"

"You like it?" Okay, I admit that I preened a little, swishing my skirt back and forth, because I loved the outfit too, and now that I was pushing forty, I'd stopped apologizing for my style and begun to celebrate it. "It's one of my favorite fit-and-flare dresses."

"The little scissors in the hat really pull the look together."

"Thanks." I touched the fascinator, securely pinned to my natural curls. "They're only a temporary addition, but it's the details that matter, right?" I wandered past her tables. "You have some truly lovely and unique things here. Are you local?"

"Thanks. Yes, I am. Well, I live in Tigard, but I do most of my business at shows like this." Dianne sat on a tall stool, her shoulders slumped. "I should have paid more attention to my booth placement." She gestured to the macrame monstrosity suspended between her and the rest of the hall. "Nobody's going to see me back here. You're only the second person who's stopped by. Even the police almost missed me."

I blinked at her. "Police?" I checked out a uniformed guy striding down the aisle. Yep, he was a cop. "Usually these events don't warrant official law enforcement. What were they looking for?"

"They didn't say. But they scared away my only customer. Not that she bought anything. She only had a chance to poke around in the embellishment jars for two minutes and flip through a handful of craft papers before, you know, the *law* arrived. I have a feeling I won't break even on this show when it's been my major income stream over the last few years."

I checked on Ava, whose stack of ink merchandise had doubled since I'd left her. "Trust me. You've got nothing to worry about. In fact, today might be your best sales day ever."

Hope flickered across Dianne's open face. "You think so?"

"Absolutely. I'm not sure why the crowd is so thin, but that's bound to change. In the meantime—" I put the jar I was still holding on her cash stand. I didn't need it, but Dianne could use the morale boost. "I'll take these. I can use them in the

Christmas Card class I'm teaching tomorrow. It's never too early to start your holiday crafting."

"Really? You teach?"

I shrugged. "It's a side gig for me. I've still got a day job that pays the bills." I made some rapid mental calculations. I could add more jewels and buttons to my card set project, give Dianne a bit of business, and maybe promote her to my students. "In fact, why don't you give me a jar of white snowflakes and a bag of gold stars."

Dianne jumped off her stool and started gathering the supplies. "Thank you. You have no idea... Do you have a flyer for your class? I can plug it during the show"—she wrinkled her nose—"assuming I get more traffic."

How about that? A new local craft supply connection *and* a check mark next to goal number three. Now all I needed was to work on goal number two, and—

"Crap!" I'd forgotten goal number one: Ava.

Dianne paused with my jars halfway in a red paisley bag. "Is something wrong?"

"Oh, sorry. Not with you. Not with these. But I've got to go. It's kind of an emergency." I backed away. Ava wasn't at the ink booth anymore—although all her bags were. "Can you hold those for me?" I fumbled a business card out of my crossbody purse and handed it to Dianne. "I really want to chat with you some more as soon as I... well..."

Dianne smiled and tucked the card into her apron pocket. "Deal with the emergency?"

"Exactly! I'll be back. I promise."

CHAPTER TWO

I hurried over to the ink booth, which was now empty except for the attendant, a balding middle-aged guy with a prosperous belly. "Do you know where my friend went"—I checked his name badge—"Fred?"

He pointed down the aisle, at the—*oh, lord*—Tim Holtz booth. "Thataway. She said you'd pick up her bags."

Of course she did. I gathered the bags from the floor, as well as the one Fred handed me, and turned to go. If Ava really got going in the Tim Holtz booth, we'd never fit all her booty in my SUV.

"Hold it," Fred said. He pointed to the ugly ink toolbox. "Don't forget that. I haven't got a bag big enough for it. Sorry."

So I hefted the thing in my arms—it was just as heavy as I'd predicted—and headed toward the danger zone.

But suddenly I was engulfed in a wave of shoppers, all with that manic crafter gleam in their eye. It was like fighting my way upstream through a leaping shoal of salmon, so I edged to the side of the aisle out of the main push. With the extra boost from my Chucks, I was tall enough to see over most heads, but Ava was shorter than PJ. I tried to catch a glimpse of her topknot, which added at least four inches to her height—really, her loctician deserved a medal, if only for dealing with Ava for as long as it must take to maintain that 'do—but the crowd was too thick. A woman in a red jersey hoodie banged into me, nearly knocking the ink toolbox out of my arms. She tugged her hood forward and growled, "Watch where you're going."

Since I was standing still, I thought she had a lot of of nerve. *I hope the stupid toolbox leaves a bruise.*

"Where the heck did all these people come from?" Two minutes ago, you could have thrown a cat through the place without hitting anything.

Then the crowd parted in front of me and PJ stood there with his rainbow-striped hand truck, thank goodness. Although he was wearing his usual casual outfit of skinny jeans with a *Star Fleet Academy Dropout* T-shirt, he'd added a bright teal feather boa to his ensemble. He pushed his glasses up and glared at me.

"LaTashia Danielle Fredericka Van Buren, if I had *known* the hysteria that would greet me at this... this... what did you call it? Cozy little craft expo?"

I smirked at him. "I may have downplayed things a bit."

"You think? I was certain the zombie apocalypse was upon us."

"Don't exaggerate." Two people next to us started fighting over the same stencil. "Okay, maybe you have a point." I nodded at his new accessory. "Nice neckwear."

"You like it?" PJ flapped the boa, sending teal feathers floating through the air to land on everyone within a three yard radius, including me. "I got it at the booth near the east entrance. She only had one this color." He batted his eyelashes. "I think it makes my eyes pop."

I pursed my lips. "PJ, your eyes are brown."

"Really, Tash, we must work on your bedside manner." He frowned at me as he plucked a teal feather off my sleeve. "What on earth are you doing? Do you imagine you're a pack mule? Because I assure you, you're not. Not in a dress that fabulous, anyway."

"I didn't have a choice, since you and your hand truck were MIA."

"Ugh, don't remind me." He took the ink toolbox. "Good grief, what is this made of? Bricks?" He set it on the flatbed cart. "The MAX train was held up *forever* outside the convention center, but that was *nothing* compared to the logjam we passed on I-5." He unthreaded each of Ava's bags from my stiff and aching fingers. "You'd think it was rush hour on the Friday before a three-day weekend instead of noon on Saturday."

I shook my hands out and flexed my fingers. The feeling might return to them presently. "Do you have any idea what the problem was?"

"None. We were all in the dark." He gestured to the surrounding crowd, lofting more teal feathers into the air. "I think most of the passengers near me were on their way here. They were all very cranky about missing the best deals."

I chuckled. "They've got good reason. Ava probably bought everything—" I stared at PJ in horror. "*Ava.* Peej, she was headed for the Tim Holtz booth."

"Dear sweet heaven," PJ muttered. "Those people can talk her into anything." He screwed up his face, making his glasses ride up his nose. "Not that it takes much talking."

"Tell me about it. I think she's already dropped at least seven hundred dollars, and she's only been to five vendors."

"Well, for pity's sake, let's find her before she buys out the entire stock of supersized holiday albums, because I may sport manly muscles in this compact frame, but even I have my limits."

He straightened his shoulders and aimed the hand cart down the aisle, but before he could mow down any wild-eyed crafters, Ava popped out of the crowd, her arms full of Tim Holtz bags.

"There you are." She piled the bags in my arms one by one although she was talking to PJ. "Poor Tash has had to carry things all over the place because you weren't here when you promised."

PJ turned his head so Ava couldn't see him roll his eyes. "There were unforeseen circumstances."

"You could have at least called," Ava scolded.

"I did." As fast as Ava dumped a bag on me, he took it and set in in the cart. "Nobody answered."

I grimaced. "Sorry. It's this exhibit hall. There's never any service in here."

Ava snorted and rolled her eyes. "If you fail to plan you plan to fail. Ooh, look, Tash. *Graphic 45!*"

PJ shook his head as the crowd swallowed her up. "What does that even mean?"

"With Ava, you never know. I think she has an endless supply of weird sayings that she whips out at random."

"Kind of like the anti-Mary Poppins." He glanced down at the cart. "Think we can find a Poppins-esque bottomless carpetbag here? 'Cause we're gonna need it if she buys much more."

I took a deep breath. "You know, Peej, I try to keep a positive attitude, but Ava is starting to get on my last nerve."

"Starting?" He flung the end of the boa over his shoulder, raising another flock of teal fluff. "Only you, with your vast ocean of patience, could have lasted this long. I'd have booted her off the Fremont Bridge the first time she *tsk*ed at me. Does Pops still ask about her?"

"Every week, without fail, although not before he asks about you." I loved how PJ claimed my grandfather and Pops claimed him right back. Seeing those two together was the picture postcard of the power of chosen family. I just wished Pops hadn't chosen Ava, too. I'd mentioned her curmudgeonly behavior to him more than once in our regular chats, but Pops had always chuckled. *"That's one of the benefits of getting old, Tashie. We've got no more rips to give."* And since Ava was partly responsible for Pops being around to *get* old, I'd deal.

PJ blew a feather off his nose. "I don't suppose you could tell Pops that the Oregon Vortex swallowed her up or that she ran off to join the circus?" He glanced sidelong at me. "Never mind.

She saved our Pops, so you'll put up with anything short of murder from her. Now me? I make no promises."

I laughed. "Planning a little retribution, are you?"

"It could happen," he said, fluttering his eyelashes, "if she steps too far out of line. Everyone knows you're the nice one and I'm *so* not. We're like sugar and... and Tabasco."

I linked my elbow with his. "Oh really? Who's the guy who keeps the office break room supplied with yummy treats?"

"Please." He stuck his nose in the air. "I could hardly eat them all myself. I'd succumb to a sugar coma, which would seriously cut into my online gaming time."

"So why make them at all?"

"Stress-baking, my angel. Blame it on my string of dreadful dates. When my prince finally comes, I'll leave our coworkers to subsist on stale Oreos and Necco Wafers from that decrepit vending machine. Now shall we reel in Ava before the weight of her purchases causes the entire state of Oregon to drop into the ocean?"

"It's a dirty job," I said.

"But somebody has to do it," we chorused.

I gestured for PJ to precede me. "Lead the way, my friend." He pushed the half-laden cart toward the Graphic 45 booth, and I chuckled as I followed him.

PJ and I had become instant besties when we'd bonded at the HR orientation at our mutual employer. He could always lift my spirits, although as I remembered exactly how many stress-baked goodies had shown up in our break room over the last couple of months, I worried that he might be hiding something from me.

Because seriously—how many bad dates could one guy have?

CHAPTER THREE

When we got to the booth, Ava was clutching no fewer than five paper packs, four chipboard sets, and three sheets of stickers—all from the new tropical island collection. She thrust them at me. "These are perfect for me to scrap my Hawaii trip."

I took them reflexively. PJ, who had stayed with the cart in the aisle, raised an eyebrow and mouthed *enabler*. "Ava, when did you go to Hawaii?"

"Well, I haven't gone yet, but you have to buy Graphic 45 when you see it otherwise it'll be sold out when you need it." She grabbed my elbow and towed me over to the woodland fairy collection, snatching the last two paper packs just as another shopper was reaching for them. "My granddaughter will love this print."

"I didn't realize you had a granddaughter." How had I missed that? "Congratulations." I mentally sorted through my own crafting supplies for an appropriate new baby card kit.

Ava added tags and a stamp set to the stack in my arms. "I don't. But my daughter is bound to get married eventually and give me grandbabies, so I need to be prepared." She charged over to the vendor, cutting off another shopper, then turned to gesture at me irritably.

I glanced sidelong at PJ. "Looks like she's ready to move on."

"Indeed. Better get cracking, Ms. Stylish Pack Mule." He brushed his brown hair back from his forehead. "Promise me we can purge this experience from our palates by indulging in the nearest happy hour."

"Not today. I've got to finish the final prep for my class. I still need to print off the student instructions, double check my supplies, and refresh my standard kit."

"Tomorrow?"

"Teaching that class." I pointed at him. "You volunteered to help, remember."

"Drat. That's right. I'd purged that momentary lapse in judgment from my memory. Then Monday after work. We will most definitely need it by then."

I joined Ava with a lighter step. Anticipating an evening out with my bestie was the perfect counter to today, and knowing PJ, he'd be totally on board with complete cocktail attire.

After Ava melted her credit card a little more, I took her firmly by the arm. "Come with me. There's a local vendor here who's got a lot of cute things I think you'll love."

"Local," she said dismissively, her tone suggesting *local* was the equivalent of *sewage*. "But, Tash, look. *Copic pens!*"

"You already have two of every color. Now come on."

Ava sighed as if she were the most put-upon person in the history of the world. "You and your love of *local*. Fine. But I won't find a thing there, I'm sure."

Uh-huh. That'll be the day. I pointed PJ toward the corner. As we threaded our way through the crowd, past the Blue Moon booth—where I nearly lost Ava to a display of Cuttlebug holiday dies—I noticed we'd picked up an entourage. Whether the shoppers trailing us wanted revenge on Ava for beating them to a treasure or were treating her like some kind of crafting truffle hound, leading them to the next gem, I couldn't tell and wasn't sure I wanted to know.

When we passed the macrame sunburst, Ava stopped stock still next to me. "Look, Tash. *Embellishments!* Why didn't you tell me?"

And she dove into Dianne's booth like she'd never seen a button or a crystal in her life.

Just in time, PJ angled the cart so it was out of the way, because the folks who'd been following us streamed into the booth and fell on Dianne's merchandise like a swarm of very artsy locusts. PJ shook his head and leaned on the cart handle. "Good grief. And I thought Andrew Christian jock sales were intense."

Even under normal circumstances, keeping embellishments neat and tidy was a challenge. With this horde pawing over everything, poor Dianne's booth was starting to look like tornado alley—and so did Dianne. Her ponytail was crooked with loose wisps of hair framing her face. Her shirt was untucked from all the people pulling and patting to get her attention. But at least she had help—another woman in a *Dianne's DooDads* apron was weighing out by-the-ounce embellishments on the little retro scale.

And despite showing a bit of wear and tear, Dianne looked *happy*. I sighed, because she was living my dream. I hoped to own my own crafting business one day and have a booth at shows like this.

Ava cut through the crowd and snatched up three of the pre-packaged rainbow mason jar sets, right out from under another patron's hand. I nearly apologized, but stopped for two reasons —first, because PJ would accuse me of being an enabler again, and second, because the crafter who got elbowed aside was that same red-hoodie person who'd bumped into me earlier.

Does it make me a bad person that I gloated a bit when she lost out to Ava? If it does, I paid for it when Ava offloaded everything onto me—those holders were made of distressed wood and they had *splinters*.

"Ava's not making any friends as usual," PJ murmured as he relieved me of the jar racks.

I plucked a sliver out of my arm. "I'm having second thoughts about that friendship myself."

Dianne met my gaze above the throng and grinned. "Hey, Tash. Don't worry. I set aside all the stuff you need for your class before the rush started."

Like somebody had hit pause, nearly everybody in the booth froze, then their heads turned toward me.

"Class?"

"Did she say class?"

"Class?"

"Unbelievable," PJ muttered. "It's like the seagulls in *Finding Nemo.*"

"Shut up and make yourself useful." I pulled a bundle of flyers out of my shopping bag and gave him half. "That's right." I had to raise my voice to be heard above a PA announcement about an upcoming vendor demonstration. "I'll be presenting a Christmas card class tomorrow at Central Paper and Supply."

"Christmas cards?" one bespectacled elderly woman said, peering at the flyer I'd handed her. "But it's June."

"It's never too early to start on Christmas cards."

"That's right," a lady in a Hello, Kitty print smock said, accepting a flyer from PJ. "I started mine in February."

"Even though we'll be focusing on a Christmas theme," I said, handing out flyers like I was dealing blackjack, "I'll teach you techniques you can use for any occasion."

The PA boomed again and this time I heard the announcement. *Dang it. The Silhouette demonstration.* I really wanted to catch that. The company had new software that allowed its machines to do fussy cutting. Seeing it in action was one of the reasons I'd been so determined to attend this show— although my resolve had wavered when Ava heard me talking about it and invited herself along.

PJ, doll that he was, must have noticed my distraction, because he took my stack of flyers. "Go do your thing. I'll stay here to flog your class and babysit Avaricious Ava."

"Are you sure?"

"Of course." He flapped the flyers at me, shooing me off. "Now go, before she dumps one of those bins into your skirt."

"Have I told you lately that I love you?" I gave PJ a hug, although I had to bend my knees to avoid smooshing his face into my boobs. *Darn these platform Chucks.*

"Back at you, babycakes. Now go. Take your time. Ava can survive without you for a while, and I'll bear up manfully."

So I hurried away and managed a front-row seat at the Silhouette demo—which resulted in me giving my own credit card a workout when I ordered one of their top-of-the-line cutting systems.

By the time I spotted PJ by the exit, I'd exceeded goal number two, adding a new Copic pen method and a Tim Holtz Distress Ink technique to the Silhouette skills—although I suppose that technically I shouldn't count the Silhouette since it wouldn't be delivered until sometime next week.

PJ trudged toward me, his cart stacked considerably higher than when I'd seen it last. "Are you sure we can't hit a happy hour somewhere? Because I definitely need a drink." He shoved his glasses farther onto the bridge of his nose. "Whoever said crafting was a *civilized* art was either lying like William Shatner's rug or seriously delusional." He shook the bedraggled ends of his boa. "Look. All those crazy crafters have flattened my feathers."

"I think it's more like you've already shed most of them. You handed out more feathers than flyers."

"Au contraire." He patted my cheek. "They snapped up every single one. If even half of them show up tomorrow, you'll have to shoehorn them into the classroom."

"I can only hope. I— Oh, drat!" I smacked myself on the forehead, nearly dislodging my hat. "I want to introduce Dianne to Graciela because I think Dianne's merchandise would do great at Central Paper, but I forgot to get Dianne's card."

"No worries. You'll see her tomorrow. She's coming to your class." He tapped the topmost bag in the cart. "Not only that, she didn't charge you for your supplies, since you were responsible for her best sales day ever."

"I think that was Ava. If she hadn't—"

"*There* you are." Ava herself marched up to us and dumped three more bags into PJ's arms. "You know, Tash, when I take you to events like this, it's a little rude for you to disappear on me."

Oooh, I was tempted, so tempted, to remind Ava whose idea this trip was. But I took the high road. "What do you say we get all this out to my car?"

As PJ was leaning over to stack Ava's latest loot on the cart, somebody barreled out of the crowd and smacked into him, sending feathers wafting into the air. I caught PJ before he could fall on his keister.

"Careful, PJ," Ava barked. "That stuff is fragile."

I glared after the person who'd run into PJ, half expecting it to be my red-hoodie nemesis, but it was a man in a leather jacket and a knitted beanie. *In June?* I mean, sure, this was Portland, but still... "This is a craft show, for goodness sake, not bumper cars."

PJ rearranged his boa. "Honey, compared to some of my dates, this was a picnic. Now, shall we go?"

CHAPTER FOUR

I ran all my classes so students only had to bring their basic craft kit, while I supplied the rest, covered by the class fee. So after the enthusiastic response at the show yesterday, I'd sat up far too late putting together more student packets—and adding some of the cute embellishments from Dianne's booth to the ones I'd already created. But I wasn't tired as I hauled one box of packets up the stairs to Central Paper's big classroom space. No, I was practically vibrating with anticipation, which made the bells on my favorite Christmas party dress (with matching fascinator) jingle all the way.

Because what if this class was the first with enough participation to launch my eventual escape from the corporate world? What if today turned out to be the foundation of my own craft business? I could only hope.

I set the box on the instructor's table next to the overhead projector as PJ hit the top of the stairs carrying the second box. He'd accessorized his prancing reindeer vest with his boa, despite its holiday-inappropriate color. He'd claimed it was for moral support.

"Are you sure I can't convince you to take the class along with everyone else?" I slid one of the packets out of the box and waggled it in the air. "I'm sure I've got enough, and as my bestie, you can't avoid crafting forever."

He gave a mock shudder and plopped his box next to the first one. "You underestimate my powers of avoidance. No."

"Why not? It's not hard. All the parts are in the packet. All you have to do is assemble it."

"Oh, sure," he said, his voice loaded with sarcasm. "No problem."

"What? It's not."

He propped his hands on his hips. "LaTashia Danielle Fredericka Van Buren, while I am not the man to back away from anything *hard*, that kit has sixteen different parts, some of them moving. Assembling it would take a high level of interest, a large dose of patience, and/or a mechanical engineering degree—all of which you have. I, on the other hand, am a systems engineer with the attention span of a gnat and a constitutional aversion to clutter."

"These don't contribute to clutter. You mail them to people on your Christmas card list."

"My particular list has zero names, so that argument won't fly either. I am more than happy to be your lovely assistant, but participate I will not. Now"—he dusted off his palms, sending teal feathers flying—"what other prep do we need?"

I gave up. PJ had resisted every single attempt I'd made to involve him in some kind of craft in the entire seven years of our friendship. That didn't mean I'd stop trying. "The tables. Let's shift them around so there's a center aisle. It's easier for me to help the students that way."

"You got it."

Graciela poked her head above the stair railing as we were pushing the last table into position. "Four more students just called to sign up for the class, *mija*. That makes twenty-two. Almost a full house."

I stood up and smoothed the ruffles on my crafting apron, the one PJ claimed made me look like a cross between a Christmas tree and Cindy-Lou Who. "Was one of them named Dianne?"

She brushed back her silver-streaked black hair. "I think so?"

"Good. She has an embellishment business, and her stuff would be perfect for the store."

Graciela's brow wrinkled. "I don't know. I'm not sure I want to expand the inventory any further."

Worry tickled my insides. Was Graciela having trouble with the store? "Well, I'm sure you'll move some of it today. My students can never resist a little shopping spree after class, and I'm expecting some walk-ins, too. There was a lot of interest at the show yesterday."

"Yes, your students never leave without buying something." She chuckled. "The way you talk up the products, I think I should pay you a commission." The door chime rang downstairs, announcing a customer. "Have a good class." Graciela waggled her fingers and disappeared down the stairs.

PJ rolled a chair from the back of the room and positioned it behind a table. "There. Seating arranged. What's next?"

"Put a class packet at each spot while I check my AV set-up?" A couple of students peered over the railing and whispered to each other. "Are you here for the Christmas card class?" They both nodded. "Then please come on up and take a seat."

"How about *I* check the AV set-up while *you* hand out packets," PJ murmured, "because I guarantee these people will ask things for which I have no answers. Besides, systems engineer, remember? I speak fluent cables and connectors."

PJ made the right call—students started to trickle in, most of them with questions about the class or crafting in general. As the time ticked closer to our one o'clock starting time, I had a respectable crowd, although not as big as I'd hoped, given my dreams of someday leaving the corporate world behind.

Dianne arrived, and I greeted her with a hug. "I'm so glad you could make it."

She chuckled. "I wasn't about to miss it. My business partner can handle the booth solo for a while today."

"Before you leave, I want to introduce you to—"

Ava pushed by Dianne, her basic kit slung across her shoulders. "This place needs an elevator."

I raised an apologetic eyebrow at Dianne and gestured for her to take an open seat.

I expected Ava to hand her kit to me, but instead she thrust it at PJ. "You're lucky I'm here. Since you abandoned me at the Expo Center yesterday, I had a good mind not to come."

"*Quelle horreur*," PJ muttered.

She pointed at the seat at the front, right next to the projector. "Put my kit over there." She held up her car keys and jingled them in his face. "There's more in the trunk." She stomped over to her seat and glared at him. "Well?"

PJ shared a bemused glance with me. "I live to serve." He trotted down the stairs as I strode to the front of the room to start the class.

"Good afternoon, everyone. I'm so glad you've joined me today. I'm Tash Van Buren, your instructor. I've put a blank table tent with each of your packets, so could you all please write your names on them and prop the tent up in front of you?" I grinned. "So much more polite to call on you by name than to point, am I right?"

"Hmmph." Ava pushed her name tent aside. "Waste of time. You already know me."

True, and I was beginning to regret it. Everybody else complied, though, including two other women from my scrapbooking circle who never missed my classes. I chuckled a bit when I noticed that all three women in the last row—the two who'd arrived first, plus another who'd slunk in at the last moment—were named Brittany.

Using a Sizzix Big Shot, I demonstrated how I'd utilized cardstock and three different die sets to make the swirling stars, Christmas trees, and wintery village silhouette included in their class packets. I handed around the sample cards I'd made to illustrate the way different embellishments could be used to alter standard die cuts, morphing them into anything from modern and whimsical to retro and traditional based on your mood or holiday theme.

After going over the basic instructions, I strolled around the classroom, answering questions and assisting the students as needed. Dianne needed no help—no surprise there. Two of the three Brittanys were having a low-voiced running commentary that included snapping multiple pictures of their cards as they worked, although the third Brittany wasn't making much progress. Neither was PJ, who was still hauling bags and boxes up from Ava's car, his expression growing more exasperated with each trip.

"Every time I walk through the store," he grumbled to me, low-voiced, "I have to sidestep this guy who's lumbering around the store like he expects it to suddenly turn into a sports bar. And he gives me a *look*." PJ sniffed. "You'd think he'd never seen a man in a boa before. Or maybe he's just envious. He's wearing a very boring and seasonally inappropriate black hoodie."

Meanwhile, Ava had spread out, encroaching on the spot next to hers with so many of the things she'd bought yesterday that it looked like she was trying to open her own craft store.

She was pawing through a cardboard box. "I know I brought those things with me. Where the heck are they?"

I moved toward her, collecting a Copic pen that had rolled down the table toward another student's workspace. "What do you need, Ava? Everything for the card should have been in your packet."

She snorted, not looking up from her search. "Your little kits are nice enough for beginners, Tash, but I like mine to make more of a statement."

I could think of a few *statements* I'd like to make, starting with the pointed toes of my red slingbacks on Ava's backside, but I didn't want to make my other students uncomfortable. If any of them thought this was what my normal classes were like, they might never come back. Several of them were already looking uneasy—the three Brittanys and a young lady in her third trimester who nervously rubbed her beautifully round belly. Dianne wasn't fazed—in fact, she sported a grin as she added red crystals to her fussy-cut holly. The two women from my scrapbooking circle seemed unconcerned, but they were used to Ava.

"What is it you're looking for, Ava?"

She poked at the card. "I want some bling for this Christmas tree. It's way too plain with those skimpy little crystals. I know I got something that would do at that show yesterday after you left me all alone."

Yes, all alone in a crowd of hundreds with PJ tagging along like her personal minion. "Maybe you can find something in my supplies. What color are you looking for?"

PJ set another box by Ava's feet. "What's the color of wretched excess?" he whispered. I glared at him, and he flung one end of his boa over his shoulder and trudged off down the stairs again.

"Red," Ava announced. "Nice, big, sparkly red. Aha!" She seized a zippered pouch out of my embellishment bin and dug out a red faceted crystal the size of my thumbnail. "This'll do." She coated the back with glue and stuck it smack in the middle of the tree. "There. Now *that's* what I'm talking about."

I suppressed a sigh and smiled at the other students. "If any of you would like different decorations for your cards, you're welcome to see if there's anything here you like better."

Dianne chuckled. "Since you got these from me, I'm not likely to complain. Besides, I've got more of them back home."

I laughed along with her as I spread the red jewels on my table next to the projector. "For those of you who don't run your own craft supply business, please help yourself."

Several women wandered up, including two of the Brittanys. One of the chatty Brittanys took several crystals and scampered back to share with her co-Brittany. The quiet Brittany peered at the sparkly red spread for several minutes, then sighed.

"Looking for something in particular?" I asked.

She flinched. "N-no. I mean, the one you gave us is fine." She trudged back to her seat as Ava leaned over and snagged another large gem.

"Next time, Tash," Ava said, "show a little more consideration for the people in your class. You'd have a better turnout if you weren't so stingy."

CHAPTER FIVE

As I strolled down the center aisle, answering questions and praising everyone's work, I checked my watch. Only fifteen more minutes left in class. Of course the students were welcome to stay if they needed a little more time, but the project wasn't complicated, despite PJ's complaints. Most of them were finishing up, other than the third Brittany, who didn't seem to have started yet. But I didn't take it personally—some people preferred to do their crafting in private. At least she'd have the kit and the instructions to take with her.

"I'll stay here in the classroom until three thirty if any of you have any questions about the materials we used, or if you'd like recommendations for any other projects. I'm pretty familiar with the inventory downstairs so I can probably lead you right to what you need."

PJ arrived with an armful of bags and set them on the floor under Ava's table. "That's the lot."

She glanced down at them. "I don't need all this. I'm done. Put that back in the car, but don't be so slow this time. I've got bingo at four over at the Elk's Lodge."

With a long-suffering sigh, PJ picked up the bags he'd just set down and stalked downstairs.

"Honestly, that boy," Ava muttered and rolled her eyes. "I'm sure he means well, but he needs to move with more *dispatch*."

One by one, the students packed up and left, most of them thanking me for the class and asking when I'd be teaching next. The talkative co-Brittanys didn't quite go that far—they kept casting nervous glances at Ava—and the third Brittany left as surreptitiously as she'd arrived. But all in all, I counted it a success, if not the life-changer I'd wished for.

While Ava was still fussing with her card, blowing on it to get the glue and paint to dry, I took Dianne downstairs to meet Graciela. Just as I'd hoped, the two of them hit it off and we chatted for a while as PJ made at least four more trips through the store and out to the parking lot, teal feathers drifting in his wake.

During his last trip, Ava was with him, head down as she pawed through her giant shoulder bag. PJ was carrying her Christmas card on his palm like an hors d'oeuvres platter and grimaced at me while he held the door for her.

I said goodbye to Dianne as he walked back in. He mock-collapsed against a shelf full of decorative stamps and wiped his brow. "Good grief, if there's a more annoying woman anywhere on the face of the earth, I don't want to meet her. In fact, I'm tempted to rid the planet of this one as a public service. Think of the pain and suffering I'd prevent."

I laughed. "Yes, but the way you dearly love to complain, wouldn't you hate to miss so many opportunities?"

He straightened up, tugging his vest like Jean-Luc Picard rising from his captain's chair, his expression thoughtful. "True. I shall shelve my homicidal thoughts for the moment."

"Good. Help me clean up?"

"Of course, my darling. I live—"

"To serve. Yes. You've mentioned it once or twice."

He grinned at me, and we left Graciela behind the cash register and headed back upstairs.

PJ grabbed the waste basket from the corner and started to clear trash off the tables. "Other than the damage to my sacroiliac and calf muscles from all the stair-climbing, I'd say your class was a resounding success."

I sighed as I turned off the projector. "I would've liked five or six more students. And there are some that I doubt will be repeat offenders."

"Nonsense. There were quite a few of them out in the parking lot, chattering away. In fact, Ava nearly mowed a straggler or two down when she peeled out of here with my black hoodie nemesis right on her tail like he was racing her to the bingo hall." He shook his head as he swept the last scraps into the trash. "He stands no chance. That woman has a lead foot. What did she do before she retired? Drive the NASCAR circuit?"

I chuckled as I bent to pick up my kit. "You know perfectly well she was a nurse. Pops's nurse."

"Nurse Ratched, maybe. Can you imagine being under her care?" He pressed his hand against his chest and staggered over to lean against the wall. "How is Pops still devoted to her?"

"Maybe she wasn't as prickly back then. She's definitely gotten worse in the last few— Oh, for Pete's sake."

"What?"

I pointed to the floor next to the projector stand. "Ava left her kit behind."

"You're kidding. I hauled a metric ton of craft supplies back and forth to her car and there's *more*?"

I lifted it up onto the table. "Well, she carried this up herself when she arrived, so it wasn't on your radar."

"You shock me, LaTashia. Ava actually carries something herself?" He peered at it, narrowing his eyes. "Why does that kit look exactly like yours?"

I huffed a breath, glaring at the bag in disgust. "Because she saw mine and liked it, so she bought one in every color they offered."

"She has bags of many colors, but she only uses the one that's your twin?" He tilted his head and tapped his chin with his index finger. "I'm sure there's something Freudian or Jungian or Behaviorist in that, but what do I know?"

He picked up the kit. "I'll take this. I'm used to the beast of burden gig by now."

But as he slung the strap over his shoulder, it broke. The bag toppled, releasing a wave of Copic pens and glue sticks to roll across the table and onto the floor. "Drat!" PJ grabbed for the bag, but only succeeded in upending it more, and the mini-mason jars from Dianne's booth tumbled out. The jar with the red embellishments lost its lid and its contents fanned out over the table.

The two of us gazed at each other, then at the spill of red buttons and bling, then back at each other.

"Do you mean to tell me," PJ said, his voice like approaching thunder, "that she had this with her *the whole time?*"

I couldn't help it—I burst out laughing. "No wonder… she couldn't… find them," I wheezed. "They were… right where they… were supposed to be."

PJ stared at me for a moment, then his lips twitched, and then both of us were hooting away like a couple of loons.

After a while, I wiped the tears from the corners of my eyes and started to scoop the embellishments back into the jar. One of the crystals was especially big and sparkly. I poked at it. "Do you suppose this is what she wanted for her card?"

PJ picked it up and tossed it in the air like he was flipping a coin. "If it was, she owes it to you to replace the one you gave her. Should I put it in your kit?"

"Of course not." I snatched it out of the air. "I can return her kit to her tomorrow at our regular scrapbooking circle. Maybe I'll mention it to her then to see if she'd like to make the offer."

He shook his head. "You will do no such thing. If I know you, you'll have given her another half dozen goodies out of your personal stash and she won't utter a word of thanks."

"Hey! You make me sound like a pushover. I'm not."

He smiled at me and took my hand. "I know you're not. But you forgive people far more times than they deserve. If it were me—"

"I know. You're Tabasco."

"Exactly."

Maybe I should channel a little bit of PJ's fire, because he was right. I'd had just about enough of being on the *forgiveness* side of the equation for folks who delayed asking for *permission*.

On the other hand, Ava never asked for permission *or* forgiveness. I eyed the crystal in my palm for an instant, almost tempted to give in to PJ's suggestion. Then I sighed and dropped it into the jar and tightened the lid.

Tomorrow would be soon enough to crack open my own personal bottle of Tabasco.

CHAPTER SIX

For some reason that I could never figure out, my boss had a sixth sense for when I had after-work plans. I was just powering down my workstation, ready to boogie out the door, when Neal poked his head in my office.

"Tash, got a minute?"

I glanced at the clock. "Actually, I don't." My scrapbooking circle meeting was due to start in less than an hour, and I couldn't stay late tonight because PJ and I were heading out to Martini Blues for our delayed post-Ava drink. In fact, PJ was driving me to Central Paper first, because my car's Check Engine light had come on as I left for work this morning. Since I never took chances with my car, I'd driven straight to my favorite mechanic, and PJ had picked me up there, transferring all my craft supplies—not to mention the garment bag with my cocktail outfit—into his MINI Clubman.

"This'll only take a second." Then Neal sat down and proceeded to drone on about the plans for the company's new community garden that was a key part of our new wellness initiative. I've told him many times that my crafting skills didn't automatically translate to gardening expertise—maintaining the Christmas cactus in my apartment and the lone echeveria on my desk was the extent of my plant care experience. But since I was so good at my unofficial role as company cheerleader, the expectation was that I would promote the garden even if I wasn't an active participant.

Whenever Neal claimed something would be quick, it always took three times as long for him to get to his point—and tonight, he didn't seem to have one.

I drummed my fingers on my leg, hidden by my desk. *Come on, Neal, get on with it.* I caught a glimpse of PJ as he strolled past my open door and made a face at Neal's back. *Rescue is at hand.*

Sure enough, thirty seconds later, my phone rang. "Pardon me, Neal, but I have to take this." I picked up the handset. "This is Tash."

"LaTashia Danielle Fredericka Van Buren, get your tushie out of there right this instant. You have *things to do,* and I am *not* missing our cocktail date because Neal insists on being tedious outside of business hours."

"Yes, Mr. Johnson, I'm sure those parts shipped this morning. I'll go check on them and call you right back."

PJ chuckled. "You're welcome. I'll meet you in the parking lot."

I hung up and collected my purse. "I'm sorry, Neal. We'll have to continue this tomorrow."

I escaped before he asked why I had to follow up on the shipment personally. For a supposedly bright guy, Neal had some very peculiar ideas about how his company actually functioned.

PJ was leaning against the MINI's rear barn doors, arms crossed. "Thank goodness." He patted the roof of the car. "Moocher and I were getting worried. I was afraid I'd have to send in the company SWAT team if Neal held you hostage much longer."

"The company doesn't have a SWAT team," I said as I maneuvered myself and my shoulder bag into Moocher's front seat.

"Clearly you've never met the night custodial crew."

When we pulled into Central Paper's little off-street lot, its double handful of parking spaces were all taken, which meant the other ladies in the scrapbooking group were already here. "Darn Neal anyway," I muttered. "You'll have to park down the street."

"Not a chance." PJ turned on his hazard blinkers. "I'll help you unload, but if you think I'm hanging around to be Ava's muscle again, you are sorely mistaken."

I peered around the lot. "I don't see Ava's car. Hmmm... she must be running late."

"Good. I'll grab your bags and deposit them at the door for you. You carry your lovely frock. That way I can make a grand escape to run a few errands before I pick you up without running the risk of getting sucked into the crafting abyss."

"Sounds like a great plan to me." Fortunately I travel lighter than Ava. We only needed one trip to get everything inside the front door. I waved at PJ and watched as Moocher pulled into traffic and zipped away.

On the one hand, I didn't mind that the lot was full—there were only five people in the circle, so if the rest of the spots were taken, it meant that Graciela had a nice bunch of customers browsing the store. With luck, that would translate into a good sales night for her.

On the other hand, I wished my crafting friends hadn't decided to be punctual for once. I liked to arrive first so I could help Graciela set up the tables and get my own projects organized before everybody else arrived to split my focus.

As I stood inside the front door, a familiar contentment warmed me from the inside. Yes, this was indeed my happy place. If only crafting could be my *paying* happy place. *Someday.*

Graciela was standing at the counter next to the cash register with several stacks of scrapbooking paper spread out in front of her. I recognized some of them—the tropical and woodland themed pages that Ava had snapped up at the show—but winced a little when I realized Graciela had shuffled them together with the Bo Bunny fall collection and plain cardstock. If Graciela had a flaw, it was in inventory control, particularly with individual pieces of paper and vellum. She'd probably lost more sales just because her customers couldn't locate the patterns and seasonal print papers they were looking for than because of lack of traffic.

She glanced up, the wrinkles smoothing out between her eyebrows. "Good evening, *mija*. Your friends have already arrived."

I caught my garment bag as it tried to slither off my arm. "Sorry I wasn't here to help you prep tonight. I got delayed at the office."

She waved my words away. "You don't have to do everything. It did the others no harm to set up for once."

I chuckled. "I suppose not. But I always like to get a head start."

"More like the chance to get something done before they all demand your attention."

Well, I couldn't say she was wrong. "Thanks again for letting us work here."

"*Pfft.*" She flapped her hands, shooing me toward the open space in the middle of the store where she let us conduct our crafting sessions. "You're good for business. The customers see you, so busy, and they want to know more. And when you show them your beautiful work?" She fanned herself with both hands. "*Aiee.* My cash register melts with all the sales."

I laughed. "I don't think it's quite that extreme, but I'm glad to help."

"Then go. Make something gorgeous." She flicked a paper pack. "Maybe with these papers so I don't have to find space for them on the shelves."

"I'll do my best." I left her scowling at her inventory once more and walked to the tables where the other ladies were setting up, hauling tonight's project tote—black nylon with *Scrap Diva* embroidered in pink—along with my garment bag and basic kit. I was halfway to to my usual table when I realized I'd left Ava's look-alike bag wedged in the back corner of Moocher. It wasn't worth calling PJ and asking him to return to the store—aside from the inconvenience, he'd probably get drafted by Ava and never get to his errands.

Oh well.

"Evening everybody. Sorry I'm late."

"Tash!" Evy Karim, an energetic sixty-year-old, jumped up from where she was unpacking her evening's project and gave me a hug. "You're allowed. Besides, I only got here a few minutes ago and Ava still hasn't arrived."

Virginia Stevens, the woman who'd been in the circle with me the longest, snorted but didn't glance up from journaling. "It's a good thing Ava's *not* here, or you'd never hear the end of it, Tash. Don't you know she's the only one who's allowed to be late?"

Nikki Papadopoulous, the youngest member of the group, just smiled at me shyly and bent her head over the Halloween wreath kit she was assembling.

Evy sat back down and continued arranging her workspace. I cringed a little when I got a good look at her supplies. Puke green and baby-poop brown. *Seriously?*

"Um, what are you working on tonight, Evy?"

She beamed up at me. Evy was a little deficient when it came to taste and skill, but she made up for it with enthusiasm and good nature. "The scrapbook for my daughter's wedding."

Oh, dear. Her daughter had gotten married in a formal Eastern Orthodox ceremony—puke and baby-poop would *not* complement the occasion. Luckily, Evy was also completely ego-free. I could suggest alternative papers—in fact, Graciela stocked some gold foil that would pick up the accents in the gorgeous church perfectly—and she'd be happy as a little crafting clam.

I sat down next to Evy and started unpacking my own project. "Nikki, did you enjoy yesterday's class?"

Nikki's head jerked up, and she scattered the contents of her wreath kit. "The class? Oh. Yes. It was good. I liked the card."

"What about you, Evy?"

"Me? Oh, sure." Evy smeared glue over the paper in an uneven swath. When she tried to position a crystal on it, though, it stuck to her finger, and she shook it until it flew off and landed on Virginia's layout. "Sorry, Virginia," she sang, then turned back to me. "But mine didn't look much like yours when I was done. I must have done something wrong."

Virginia removed Evy's errant crystal with a pair of long-nosed tweezers. "At least you didn't plunder Tash's supplies to finish it like Ava did."

I paused, my scrapbook half out of its tote. "You weren't at the class, Virginia. How'd you find out that Ava borrowed an embellishment from me?"

"Borrowed?" Virginia snorted again. "Hardly. Evy told me all about it, and commandeered is what I'd call it." She pointed the tweezers at me. "Do you remember those typewriter font stamps I told you about at last week's session? The discontinued ones I *finally* found on Etsy?"

"Uh-huh." I spread out the pictures from last year's Icelandic vacation. "Did you get them? They sounded lovely."

"No, I didn't. Because little Miss *Ava* skedaddled out of here early and snapped them out from under me—and then *flaunted* them in front of me. I could have strangled her." Virginia flung her tweezers onto the table. "She knew I wanted them. She heard me say so. She wouldn't even have known about them if not for me, and she'll probably never even use them. She'll stick them in that overstocked room of hers and forget all about them."

One of the customers had wandered over. She peered over Evy's shoulder and then backed away, out of earshot, her eyes wide. *Just as well.* Graciela wouldn't thank us for talking smack in the middle of her store during business hours.

Time to change the subject. I cleared my throat. "Well, I'm finally getting around to scrapping my Iceland trip."

"Oooh." Evy wiggled in her seat, scattering glitter from the small tube in her hand. "Do we get to see the pictures of your Viking?" She batted her eyelashes. "Bee-*yorn*?"

"Not tonight." In fact, I was editing Bjorn out of my vacation scrapbook entirely. Some of the pictures he sent me were *not* safe for public viewing—even *I* didn't want to view them. *Ugh.* Men could be so weird.

"If I convince my hubby to take me to Iceland for our anniversary," Evy said, "do you think I could have a Viking fling too?"

I raised my eyebrows. "Wouldn't that put a crimp in your anniversary celebrations?"

Evy waved her hand in a pooh-pooh gesture. "He won't mind. He'll be too busy fishing."

"Well, Bjorn is yesterday's news." Our very brief romance had started out so promising, too. He was tall, strong, had a great laugh. Unfortunately, some of the things he chose to laugh *at* did *not* align with my core values. I raised my wrist and did the princess wave so they could check out the sparkle. "Although I have to give him props for his apology gifts."

Evy's eyes rounded. "A diamond tennis bracelet?" she squeaked. "I *definitely* want my own Viking."

"If I recall much about Vikings," Virginia said, positioning some ribbon across the middle of her two-page spread with pinpoint accuracy, "they'd be more likely to give you a herring than diamonds."

Evy wrinkled her nose. "Well, that's no good. I can get *that* from my hubby. Maybe I'll plan a staycation instead." Her expression brightened. "It'll give me a chance to catch up on my scrapbooking."

"Heaven help us all," Virginia murmured, low enough that Evy couldn't hear. "That's enough to turn *anyone* homicidal."

CHAPTER SEVEN

As I tried to decide between two photographs of the Blue Lagoon, I caught sight of my wristwatch. It was already 7:00. "Did Ava tell any of you that she was going to be late? Or that she planned on skipping tonight?"

Nikki shook her head, and then hunched over her wreath, although she didn't seem to be making much progress—she'd been fussing with the same paper candy corn since I'd arrived.

"Not me." Evy peered at her page, where she'd accidentally —or maybe it was on purpose—scrawled something in purple archival ink in a crooked swath. "Rats."

Virginia set her finished layout aside and reached for a new page. "You're the one she talks to, Tash."

Virginia had a point. I hadn't noticed any texts, but then I kept my personal cell phone on silent at work, and after Neal ambushed me, I hadn't checked for messages in my rush to get here.

I pulled out my phone, but the only text I had was from PJ with a picture of perfectly baked cream cheese brownies. *He's stress baking now? How did he manage to squeeze in a bad date since he dropped me off?* I set that thought aside and dialed Ava's number.

"No answer." I sent her a quick text, then put my phone away. "She's not required to be here. Something probably came up."

"Yeah," Virginia muttered as she sorted through her bag of cardboard lettering. "She's probably hijacking somebody else's hard-won discovery. Snatching something else she's not entitled to."

Nikki's hand jerked, and she knocked her unassembled cutouts on the floor. "Sorry." She slid off her chair, then gathered them into her shirt tail.

"Even though Ava doesn't *have* to report in," Evy said, "it would have been polite. Especially to you, Tash."

"Me?" I stopped in the middle of wiping fingerprints off the pictures on my own finished spread. "She doesn't owe me anything either."

"No, but she acts like you owe *her*. She treats you and that cutie-patootie friend of yours like you're nothing more than her minions. That's not right."

I eyed the customers still browsing the aisles. Some of them had started to approach us, but then veered off when they heard the personal—and not very charitable—chitchat.

I took a deep breath and leaned forward. "What's not right," I said, keeping my voice low, "is for us to gossip and drag people in the middle of Graciela's store. I come here to forget about all the negativity in the world and at work. To decompress." I tapped my scrapbook. "To accomplish something lasting, something meaningful to me or to someone I care about. So I suggest we focus on that. On our goals for tonight." I straightened up and pressed my palms against the table. "My goal is to complete at least three spreads for my Iceland adventure—sans Bjorn. Virginia?"

She pursed her lips, tilting her head as she considered the work she'd already completed. "My goal is to finish journaling my great-grandfather's early years in Germany and start the calligraphy for his marriage certificate page. It would be a lot easier to do my picture captions if I had those typewriter stamps, but I'll have to make do."

I turned to Nikki, who was still kneeling on the floor. "What about you, honey? What do you want to accomplish this evening?"

"I, um, need to use the restroom." She stood up and stumbled toward the back room, a jumble of orange and black supplies nestled in her shirt.

"Well, I suppose that counts as an accomplishment." Virginia craned her neck to peer at Nikki's project. "She certainly hasn't done much else."

"The evening's young," I said. "Let's get to work."

One of the customers edged over to my table. "Oh, that's lovely. I would have never thought of putting a map of a city with my vacation pictures."

I smiled up at her. "That's part of the fun. Finding ways to combine unexpected things and make them more than the sum of their parts."

She glanced at Evy's page—which now sported neon orange ribbon to complement (or not) the puke, poo, and purple. "Um. That's, er, very nice too."

Evy beamed at her. "Isn't it? If you like, I can teach you how to do it yourself."

"No. No, thank you." She peered at the iridescent vellum I was using to represent snow. "Do you suppose there's more of that paper here in the store?"

"I'm sure of it. Let me show you." I walked her over to the paper racks and left her trying to decide between a matte and a high gloss finish.

The gold paper caught my eye. "Evy, honey? I've got an idea for your wedding book. Could you come over here for a sec?"

I managed to get Evy situated with some more appropriate wedding-themed supplies, although in the process I laid my hand in a puddle of glue and glitter. "Drat. I need to go wash this off."

Virginia set aside her calligraphy to dry. "While you're there, you'd better see if Nikki fell in."

Startled, I glanced at Nikki's empty chair. "She's not back yet?" It had been at least twenty minutes, maybe half an hour. I hoped she was okay. She'd seemed even more skittish than usual this evening. I left Evy humming over her new paper—*I hope she doesn't slather it with chartreuse paint while I'm gone*—and Virginia attacking another page of journaling with her usual single-minded intensity, and headed into the back room.

I actually loved the store's back room—the overstock stacked on shelves, the boxes of new shipments waiting to be unpacked, the stairs leading up to the classroom where I spent so many wonderful hours, both as a student and a teacher. True, it could use a bit more storage, and it could definitely do without the broken-down orange sofa, but it still filled me with a weird combination of comfort and longing.

The first floor restroom was behind a row of shelves that blocked the rear quarter of the room, currently jammed with decorations for a dozen different holidays. Above a nodding 3D Santa, I could see that its light was out and its door open. Had Nikki gone upstairs to use the restroom outside the classroom? I skirted the shelves and headed for the stairs, but stopped with one foot on the first step.

Nikki was standing in front of a file cabinet, one hand holding a small bag of what I recognized as tiny 3D Easter egg embellishments, the other rifling through an open drawer.

"Nikki?"

She slammed the drawer shut and whirled, dropping the bag and sending tiny Easter eggs skittering over the floor. She put her hands behind her back. "I was just looking."

"Oookay." I moved closer, sidestepping the stuff on the floor. "If you need holiday embellishments that aren't on the floor, I'm sure Graciela can dig some out for you."

"Oh. No. I don't… That is I won't…" She swallowed audibly and stared down at her feet.

"Nikki?" I kept my voice soft. "Is something wrong? Were you upset by the gossip?"

Her chin jerked up. "Wh-what?"

"The things that were said about Ava. Did that bother you?"

"No." She looked down again, drawing a circle on the linoleum tiles with the toe of her sneaker. "I mean sort of."

I sighed. Nikki was so much younger than the rest of us. Folks complained that young people these days are so cynical, but to me, Nikki seemed even younger than my ten-year-old niece. Innocent. Naive. Or maybe just sheltered. *Or maybe it's just that she's so much smaller than me.* She was a little wisp of a thing, really.

"I can say something to them if you want. Remind them of the need to be kinder if you—"

"No!" Her shoulders hunched, and she drew in on herself. "That would be wor—" She swallowed again. "They said those things about Ava. But Ava talks about people too. Um…" Her glance flickered to my face and away. "About you. About your friend."

I clenched my jaw. *I am definitely having* words *with Ava when she decides to show up.* "You don't need to repeat anything. I'm sure I can guess."

"But… but if they say those things about people who are their friends, who haven't done anything wrong…" She screwed up her face. "Okay, maybe Ava's done *some* things wrong, but you haven't. If they say those things about you, what would they say about somebody who's done something *really* bad?"

A frisson crept up my spine. *A goose walking over my grave,* my grandmother would say. "What kind of thing?"

"Just, um, things."

I took a step closer. "Is there something you want to talk to me about, Nikki?"

"What? No. Um, never mind. I need to get back to my project." She scurried out.

I huffed out a breath, studying the mess around my feet. *Can't very well leave this lying around.*

I hustled over to the restroom to wash my hands, then returned to gather up the scattered mess. I eyed the file cabinet. Which drawer was Nikki poking around in? I pulled out the top drawer. Nope. This one was full of store records, not out-of-season stock.

I was about to close the drawer when something caught my eye in a half-open file folder—a big red *Past Due* stamp.

A whole flock of geese must be marching across that graveyard, because I shuddered again. Surely the store wasn't in trouble, was it? It seemed busier than ever these days. Maybe that was an old invoice, from years ago. Otherwise why would it be out here in no-man's-land?

Of course, Graciela didn't have an office per se—there was a room that was supposed to be an office, but she used it to store extra chairs for the classroom.

Feeling ten kinds of creepy, I teased the file folder open a little wider and checked the date on the invoice.

It was from April of this year.

I slid the drawer closed, wincing at the *snick* of the latch. Graciela wouldn't thank me for snooping in her files, but I was glad I'd discovered the problem. If Central Paper was in trouble, then it was up to me, to the people like me who found a haven here, to make sure it got *out* of trouble. And for that, it needed better stock management, inventory that moved—I glowered at the file cabinet with its unsold seasonal items—but above all, it needed customers. So I'd do everything in my power to make sure it got them.

After I tidied up the spill, I squared my shoulders and headed back onto the floor. And if I spent more time chatting up customers for the rest of the evening and helping them find supplies for their projects instead of working on my own? Well, I was only doing my part.

CHAPTER EIGHT

At precisely 7:59, PJ sailed through the door and struck a pose. He was wearing a vintage black double-breasted suit, a black fedora, and his boa. "Hello, ladies," he said, trying—not very successfully—to match the voice of that yummy man in the Old Spice commercials.

I was helping a customer choose a Christmas-themed die. She edged toward me. "Is he somebody?" she whispered out of the corner of her mouth. "He looks like somebody."

"Oh, he's somebody, all right." The best friend I'd ever had, but I doubted that's what she meant. PJ would be thrilled with her reaction, though. Bemoaning his thirty-something white-guy averageness—medium brown hair, medium brown eyes, *medium* size—he always tried to counter it with a little extra flair whenever we went out, although he never went too far overboard. He claimed there was no point: *"LaTashia Danielle Fredericka Van Buren, there's zero chance of anyone noticing me, even if I were stark raving nude. Not when you sashay in wearing one of your swing skirts and a beehive wig."*

Not that I'd be wearing that particular wig tonight. It didn't go with my black *Breakfast at Tiffany's* cocktail dress, plus that wig would never fit in Moocher. I'd have to cut a hole in the roof and PJ certainly wouldn't want a permanent sunroof in rainy Portland.

"Hi, PJ," Evy caroled. "Come see my scrapbook. Tash helped me."

PJ flung the end of his boa over his shoulder—Graciela shook her head at the teal feather fallout—and sauntered over to the table. His eyes widened behind his glasses when he saw the puke-poo-purple monstrosity on the corner of the table. "Tash helped you with that?"

Evy chuckled. "Oh, not that one. But my niece graduated from OSU last month. It'll do for that, don't you think?"

"Charming," PJ murmured faintly.

Oh, lord. Adding OSU orange and black to puke-poo-purple? Somehow I'd talk her out of it, or her niece, a perfectly lovely girl who'd attended several of my classes, would never forgive me.

As Evy displayed the wedding album for PJ's somewhat pained inspection, I helped the customer gather the last of her supplies and escorted her to the cash register. *There.* That made the eighth person I'd walked through a project. Six of them— three birthday cards, a celebration of life memorial poster, and a Cuttlebug sale to a bride-to-be—had all happened in rapid succession. I hadn't finished my own pages, but I'd contributed to Graciela's bottom line for the day, which was more important.

As I'd played a combination of docent, craft counselor, and supply upseller, though, I'd kept an eye on Nikki. She'd spent most of the evening digging through her kit, although not very constructively since she never seemed to take anything out of it. The rest of the time, she'd watched Virginia put together another of her technically perfect but artistically bland genealogy pages.

Graciela bagged up the customer's purchases and sent her out the door with a smile. Then she hustled out from behind the counter and gave me a hug. "I should pay you a commission. You sold *three* Cricuts, that Cuttlebug, and an easel that's been gathering dust for months, not to mention all the paper, adhesives, and embellishments. *Thank* you."

I patted her back. "I like helping people. No need for thanks." *Just please keep the store open.*

"You help so many. Who helps you?"

"Oh, everyone does. I've got no complaints." Well, other than wrangling Ava, or when Neal showed up at quitting time with one of his *quick questions.*

PJ joined us at the counter. "Do you really intend to wear *business* attire to Martini Blues? That is so not like you, LaTashia."

"You know I don't. You helped stow my garment bag in Moocher this morning."

He clasped both hands under his chin. "Please tell me you brought the *Breakfast at Tiffany's* one."

"Absolutely."

"Excellent." He waggled the end of his boa. "It will go *perfectly* with my neckwear du jour."

I quirked one eyebrow. "You're wearing a tie *and* a boa. Isn't that a little overkill? Or is this the latest trendy look?"

He reared back in mock outrage. "It's not *trendy*. It's *style*."

Graciela and I both chuckled. "Oh, pardon me."

"Go." He took my arm and aimed me for the back room as the door chimed behind me. "Change. Hurry, or we'll miss all the best olives."

"You'd better contain your stylish neckwear or you'll end up with feathers in your martini."

"A small price to pay for fabulousity. Now shoo."

When I got back to our tables, Nikki's workstation was clear. "Did Nikki leave already?"

Virginia looked up from packing her kit with mathematical precision. "Yes. I'm surprised she didn't say goodbye. She walked right past you."

That must have been the door chime I'd heard. *Drat.* I'd wanted to make sure she was okay. Oh well. I'd give her a call later to check in on her.

Evy surveyed the shambles on the table in front of her. "Oh, dear. I don't understand how you two always manage to stay so *neat.*" She sighed and began shoving her supplies haphazardly into her totes. I forced myself to turn away. *Not my projects. Not my problem.* I couldn't fix all of Evy's missteps, and I shouldn't really try. After all, the point of doing handcrafts was to *do* handcrafts. Evy truly enjoyed the process, and even if her end products weren't something that I'd create, they made her happy, and that was all that mattered.

I retrieved my garment bag from where I'd draped it over a chair but didn't even bother with the tiny first floor washroom. This dress needed some extra special wiggling, so I headed upstairs to change in the larger restroom next to the classroom.

I unzipped the bag and—I admit it—I squealed. I couldn't help it. I loved how this black sheath hugged my curves and showcased my back and shoulders. I silently thanked heaven for the invention of adhesive bras and Spanx as I slid into my dress. The thigh-high slit made stockings a moot point, but my legs were one of my best features anyway—or so PJ said. *"You've got legs that look like they do something, LaTashia. Smooth, shapely, and sturdy, like an Amazon general."*

I fluffed out my natural curls so I'd have dramatic big hair and clipped a rhinestone-encrusted barrette to one side. The diamond stud earrings I'd bought myself to match the tennis bracelet added a classically elegant touch. A quick touch-up of my makeup with a glossy red lip tint and I was almost ready for the evening.

I had to take off Bjorn's apology bracelet to work my fingers into my black satin cocktail gloves. Then I couldn't fasten it again—the gloves looked fabulous, but they severely limited my dexterity. So I packed my work clothes into the garment bag, picked up the bracelet, slipped on my heels, and glided downstairs.

PJ was standing in the middle of the stock room, frowning at the awful orange sofa, but he looked up when I was halfway down. "Ooh la la."

I handed him the bracelet. "Fasten this for me?"

"Ah, the Diamonds of Despair. A nice touch." He bent his head over my wrist, the brim of his fedora brushing my bare shoulder.

"If you're suggesting that I regret kicking Bjorn to the curb—"

"Not *your* despair, darling. *His.* Because this little token of his affection didn't result in you throwing caution—not to mention your wits, your joy, and your self-respect—to the wind and agreeing to date him again." He patted my wrist. "There. And the next time you wing off on vacation without me, remember: Never date anyone named for somebody in ABBA."

He turned in a flurry of fluff and stalked out of the room, humming "Waterloo." He collected my totes and kit. "Nobody wearing *that* dress, not to mention the Diamonds of Despair, should carry anything as mundane as a craft tote." He peered at the pink embroidery. "Not even one as fabulous as this."

Graciela locked the door behind us when we stepped out into the cool June evening. It was still light—the days leading up to the solstice were long up here north of the forty-fifth parallel—although it would be dark by the time we reached the club. My black patent stilettos weren't made for long hikes, but luckily Moocher was parked in the spot nearest the sidewalk.

"I still can't believe we fit all my stuff in Moocher. It's not like it has a cavernous trunk."

"It's not a trunk. It's a *tonneau.*" PJ lifted his chin. "And I'll have you know that Moocher is *quite* spacious."

"Uh-huh. Tell that to my beehive wig. If I hadn't skootched down in the seat last weekend—which was *not* comfy—it would have been mooshed beyond recognition."

"Let me rephrase. Moocher is quite spacious for *reasonable* use." He opened the double doors to Moocher's hind end—trunk, *tonneau*, or whatever. "Your wig collection is many things, LaTashia, but I doubt anyone would characterize it as *reasonable*."

I was about to sling my garment bag on top of my totes when I saw it. "Drat. I forgot we still had Ava's kit."

PJ frowned at it. "I'd have thought she'd have summoned me to return with her *prrrrecious* the instant she spied the whites of your eyes."

I shrugged. "She wasn't here." Come to think of it, I still hadn't heard from her. It was probably just as well she'd been a no-show—she wouldn't have been able to resist commenting on Evy's puke-poo-purple page, and her snide remarks always made Nikki even more nervous. "If you don't mind, I'd like to drop it off at her place on the way to Martini Blues. It's not far."

He eyed me. "The chances of you escaping from Ava in under half an hour are precisely nil—if you escape at all. Let the record show that I think this is a terrible, no good, very bad idea." He closed up the back and stalked to the passenger door to open it for me. "And if I'm right, the first round of drinks is on you."

I patted his shoulder. "I promise. I'll only take a minute. You can even leave the car running."

"Excellent." He held my elbow to steady me while I lowered myself onto the seat. "One of my boyhood dreams was to grow up to be a getaway driver."

CHAPTER NINE

When we pulled up in front of Ava's gingerbread Victorian, the house was almost completely dark, only a faint glimmer of light in an upstairs window. I peered at the dim porch. "It doesn't look like she's home. She must have had plans with other friends tonight."

"Ava has other friends?" PJ muttered.

I ignored him as he turned off the car. "I know where she keeps the spare key. I can just run the kit up to her craft room and text her that I was here." I poked him in the arm. "See? No martini delay at all."

"I'll believe it when I see it. She probably has an android replica. Lots of them. Like Stella Mudd in that *Star Trek TOS* episode with all the twins in it."

I laughed and opened my door. "You're such a geek."

"Excuse me? Do I need to remind you which one of us has a larger-than-life oil painting of Lieutenant Uhura in the living room, because it ain't me, babe." He climbed out of the car. "It takes a geek to know a geek."

"Uh-huh." I circled to the rear doors, but PJ beat me to it.

"Allow me." He retrieved Ava's kit. "After all, I was the pack mule of choice yesterday."

We picked our way up the flagstone path and mounted the porch stairs, PJ steadying me with a hand on my elbow—not that I needed it, but it was a nice gesture. I reached up, patting along the door frame where Ava kept her spare key despite multiple warnings from both her daughter and me.

"Uh, Tash?" PJ's voice wobbled. "I don't think we need the key. The door's open."

"What?" I let my arm drop, the Diamonds of Despair falling to rest at the base of my thumb. Sure enough, the door wasn't latched. "Drat Ava. It's bad enough she leaves her key in such an obvious place, but she really should learn to close her freaking door! This is a nice neighborhood, but still."

PJ clutched my arm. "Oh my god, this is like the biggest horror movie cliché *ever*."

"Would you prefer to stay out here? I can take this in myself."

"Are you kidding? This is my chance to live my B-Movie dreams!"

Yep, in addition to being a total sci-fi geek, PJ was hopelessly addicted to bad horror movies—the cheesier they were, the better he liked them. He kept threatening to make me put together a scrapbook for him with pictures from the worst creature special effects from all his favorites.

He was joking of course, but I had news for him—I was actually doing it! It was going to be one of his Christmas gifts this year.

I pushed open the door which creaked ominously.

"Perfect," PJ breathed. The ends of his boa were quivering.

"Ava, honey?" I called. "Are you here?"

"Bum bum *bum*."

I elbowed PJ in the ribs. "I can do without the scary movie soundtrack."

"I've got the shrieking violins from *Psycho* on my phone, if that would be better. I use it for my boss's ringtone."

"No, thanks." I stepped into the darkened vestibule. The only light in the place was bleeding down the stairs. I crept toward them, PJ glued to my side. "Looks like the light might be coming from her craft room," I whispered. Icy fingers crawled up my spine. I elbowed PJ again. "Now you've got me doing it. There's nothing sinister about this."

"No? We're inside Ava's house. That's sinister enough for me. But stumbling around in the dark is a little much." He strode over to the wall between the kitchen and living room archways and flicked on the lights, causing me to blink in the sudden glare. "There." He propped a hand on the doorway trim and peered into the kitchen. "She has a 'Tea for Two' painting just like yours."

"It was a class project."

He goggled at me over his shoulder. "You mean she actually finished a project?"

"No." I pressed the cool satin of my gloves against my heated cheeks. *This is stupid. Why am I embarrassed?* PJ was well aware of my history with Ava's *craftus interruptus*. "I, um, may have put the final touches on it."

He turned on the kitchen light and crossed to the wall to peer at the artwork. "Finishing touches, huh? This is a minimum 80% Tash creation. I recognize this. And this." He pressed his fingertip against each telltale swirl and strategic paint splatter in turn. "And these too."

I heaved a sigh. *The things I do for Pops.* "Trust me. It was easier than hearing about how impossible the class was."

"Did any of the other students have trouble?"

"Of course not." I smoothed my gloves over my wrists. "Now let's get this over with. I thought you were in a hurry to get to that first martini."

"That was before we stepped into *Nightmare on*— What's the name of this street?"

"Heron Swallow."

He tapped his chin. "*Nightmare on Heron Swallow*? That sounds more porn-ish than horror-ific. The scriptwriter should be shot. Or perhaps stabbed repeatedly. But you make an excellent point." He marched to the staircase, but he'd barely put a foot on the first step when a multicolored blur shot down the stairs.

PJ hollered something about aliens and I might have shrieked just a bit. I pressed a hand to my chest and caught my breath. Then tried not to laugh.

"It's just Ava's cat."

The fluffy little calico was bouncing at the foot of the stairs, fur standing up along her spine, her back and tail arched like an old man's eyebrows.

He leaned over, his boa dangling in front of him, and squinted at her. "Are you sure it's not an alien?"

"Positive." Because my nose was already twitching. My feline allergy was one of the reasons I'd never accepted any of Ava's repeated invitations to work in her craft room. Well, that, and I had no desire to subject myself to more one-on-one Ava time, my debt to her for Pops's care notwithstanding.

The cat took a swipe at PJ with one orange paw. "I think she hates me."

"It's not you. It's your boa." Sure enough, the cat batted at the boa again, the fur on her tail flattening.

He snatched it out of her reach. "Well, she can't have it." He straightened up. "Stop dawdling, LaTashia. Let's get this show on the road."

He pivoted and marched three steps up the stairs but then stopped and looked over his shoulder at me. His grin in the wan light made him look like a demented jack-o'-lantern. In a fedora. "What am I thinking? We can't squander an opportunity this golden, furry, feather-phobic aliens notwithstanding." He crouched down and clutched the banister. "I'm sure that last creature was only a scout," he whispered, "the smallest of the species. When we locate the nest, we're bound to run into the guards and—" He turned to face me, taking the next step backwards. "—the *queeeeeeen.*"

Shivers raced across my skin. "Will you stop it? Let's just drop the kit and go."

Of course, now that PJ had buried himself in the part, he ignored me. He hugged the kit to his chest and continued up the stairs. "You're mad, I tell you, mad. This sacred artifact is our only hope." He reached the top of the steps and crept toward the open craft room door. "It contains ancient secrets, the key to defeating the hive and saving our world from certain destruction!"

I laughed shakily. "Ava's kit is hardly sacred, and the most ancient thing in it is a set of last year's Graphic 45 safari stickers."

PJ closed his eyes and pinched the bridge of his nose. "Tash, you are simply *not* immersing yourself in this experience."

"I'd prefer to immerse myself in a martini flight." I pointed a gloved finger at him. "And if Ava gets home and catches us here, we could be stuck here for hours with nothing to drink but her homemade wine."

PJ's eyes popped wide, his glasses glinting in the side-light as he shuddered. "Yeesh. Now *that* is truly horrifying. Even *I* can't justify it with a little impromptu cosplay." He turned and headed for the craft room. "Let's drop this thing and—*oh my god.*"

I glared at him and stomped up the stairs. "I thought we were done playing write-your-own-horror-movie. I swear, PJ, if you don't stop—"

"No, Tash. Really." He pointed a shaking finger at the open door. "Somebody's tossed the place."

"What?" My voice came out in a squeak.

"I mean it. There's crap *all over.*"

Goosebumps lifting on my arms, I rushed to peer over his shoulder. But at the state of the room, I let out a shaky laugh. "Yeah. Somebody being Ava."

PJ's jaw sagged. "You're joking. *This* is how she takes care of her stuff?"

"'Fraid so." Ava's craft room had started out as an HGTV dream, but every time her stock outgrew her storage, she grafted yet another organizational system onto it. Now it was more like a nightmare, with overfull cheap plastic bins stacked atop the gorgeous antique table, crooked particleboard boxes shoved onto the custom-built shelves, and old plastic yogurt containers fighting for space with vintage mason jars on the repurposed country hutch. The sight always made me wince, which was another reason I never accepted Ava's crafting invitations.

She managed to keep it marginally neat most days—not as regimented as Virginia's space, but then nobody's was, not even mine. Today wasn't one of those days, however, because the counters were awash in glitter tubes and loose card stock, and the floor was littered with embellishments, craft tools, dies, and stamps. Half the drawers sagged open, and a Cuttlebug tilted precariously off the top of the hutch.

"This isn't unusual. I've seen it worse."

PJ stalked into the room and the breeze of his passing set discarded bags dancing across the floor. "I'm outraged." PJ nudged an empty red bag—the one from Dianne's DooDads—with his toe. "I schlepped this bag from one end of the Expo Center to the other, not to mention hauling it up and down Central Paper's stairs yesterday at least a dozen times, and now she just tosses it aside as if it were garbage. Where's the consideration? Where's the respect?"

"Well, it *is* garbage, or at least recycling. Besides, you only carried it up once and down once." I righted one of the mason jars stuffed with Copic markers on the counter. "Don't exaggerate."

"Well, it *felt* like dozens of times." He scooped up two empty jars and set them on the window sill. "And I don't exaggerate. I engage in hyperbole." He shoved the Cuttlebug more securely onto the hutch before it could fall off and brain him. "Just *look* at this place. With all the sparkly rainbow, er, rain, it looks like the aftermath of a Pride parade." PJ picked up an intricate silver snowflake die between a thumb and forefinger. "Although I prefer my Pride events with fewer pointy bits. Somebody could put their eye out with this. It's like some kind of... of crafter shuriken." He gingerly set it on overcrowded shelf.

"I expect she was looking for something. Probably her kit."

PJ loosened his boa where it had tightened around his throat, adding teal feathers to the chaos. "What are the odds she'll blame you for the mess she made trying to find it?"

"Me?" I fluttered my eyelashes at him. "I wasn't the one who missed it dozens and dozens of times while carting bags up and down the stairs."

He frowned at me. "Don't exaggerate, LaTashia. I am *very* detail-oriented. I wouldn't have missed it if it hadn't been hiding. Probably on purpose. Camouflaging itself by masquerading as *your* bag." He held the kit out and shook it. "It's not a sacred object that will save the world at all. In fact, it's probably the secret weapon that will totally destroy life as we know it."

"In that case, why not offload it before you accidentally set it off?"

He blinked at me. "Good point. We have no idea what the detonation mechanism is." He glanced around, but there wasn't a clear surface anywhere in the room. "Where do you suggest I put it? Is there a spare nuclear containment unit in here somewhere?"

"Just put it in the closet. I'll write her a note to let her know we were here."

"A note? Why not just text her?"

I gave him a *seriously?* glare. "Because then she'd text me back and demand that we wait for her."

"Ah. Yes. Well, we wouldn't want that." He chuckled. "You know, if this really *were* one of those gloriously cheesy seventies horror movies, this is where we'd discover the body." He lifted his feet in exaggerated—okay, hyperbolic—steps while I tried to find a working pen amid the mess on the counter. "Slowly he turned. Step by step. Inch by inch."

"Shut up, you goof. I'd really like to get out of here before Martini Blues closes."

"I can be efficient *and* entertaining at the same time." He eyed the closet door. "I just hope the closet is more organized than the rest of the room or I won't be able to shove the doomsday device in without a matter compressor."

I looked up from my search. "Do you want me to do it?"

"No, no." He made shooing motions with one hand and tucked the alleged doomsday device under his other arm. "Carry on with your knitting. Send in the search dogs—or perhaps a yummy firefighter or two—if I don't emerge by Christmas."

I chuckled and turned back to the disarray of Ava's work table. "If I were a working gel pen," I murmured as the closet door creaked open behind me, "where would I be?"

"Uh, Tash?"

"Hmmm?" I moved a stack of craft magazines and uncovered a purple pen. "Aha!"

"There's a body."

CHAPTER TEN

"There's *what*?" I flung the pen down and hurried to PJ's side, crunching buttons and crystals under my patent leather toes.

"One of those shuriken thingies is sticking out of her neck." He pointed, his face whiter than I'd ever seen it, then grabbed my hand, his grip so tight it was almost painful.

There, on the floor of the surprisingly neat closet, lay Ava, facedown, her locs askew, red staining the white carpet under her head. A snowflake die protruded from the angle of her jaw.

I let go of PJ's hand and fumbled for my cocktail purse, nearly snapping its delicate strap when I pulled out my phone.

"What are you doing?" PJ's voice seesawed—or else my hearing had gone wonky with shock.

"Calling 9-1-1." But with my satin gloves on, I couldn't activate the touch ID. I bit the end of one glove finger and yanked at it with my teeth.

PJ smacked my hand away. "Are you kidding? I've watched *dozens* of episodes of *Forensic Files*. The person who makes the 9-1-1 call is *always* the murderer."

"Honey, calling 9-1-1 doesn't *make* you the murderer. The killers on *Forensic Files* are just stupid."

"I know. I know. But—"

"Peej. We need to do this." I could tell there was very little chance that Ava was alive, but we still needed to get the first responders here.

He gulped, but nodded and helped me take off my glove.

"9-1-1, what's your emergency?"

"I just found my friend face down in her closet. I think she's dead."

"Where are you?"

I gave her Ava's address, then took a few deep breaths to try to calm my nerves. My hands were shaking, and I leaned against the wall for support. The operator clicked away on her keyboard in a rapid fire pattern that might have been soothing under different circumstances.

"Don't hang up. Stay on the line with me. Help is on the way." Her tone was practiced and reassuring, and the tension in my shoulders eased. "What is your name?"

"LaTashia Van Buren. We just swung by to drop off her craft kit because she didn't show up for our usual scrapbooking circle. We meet twice a month at Central Paper and Supply in downtown Beaverton. If you're a crafter, you should check it out." I forced myself to stop talking. Even when I was little, talking was my way of coping with nervous energy. Now was most definitely not the time to promote Graciela's store. PJ swiveled his head back and forth between me and the body as if willing me to sprinkle some fairy dust and cause Ava to magically arise.

"Is she breathing?" The operator's voice sliced through my meandering thoughts.

Ava wasn't moving at all that I could see, but I met PJ's wide, panicked gaze. "Could you check to see if she's breathing? I can't kneel down in this dress."

His breath hitched. "You want me to *touch* her?"

"Ma'am," the 9-1-1 operator said, "do you have someone there with you?"

"Yes. Another friend. He's actually the one who found the body." I squeezed PJ's shoulder. "I'm sorry, honey, but you have to." PJ might be addicted to true crime TV and crappy horror movies, but I doubted he'd ever witnessed death personally. "I'd do it if I could."

"Right." His voice was thready. "Yes. I can do it." He lowered himself toward Ava's body.

"PJ. Your boa."

"Oh my god!" He caught its tails just as they were about to brush Ava's out-flung arm, his throat working. His face was nearly the same color as his feathers as he reached out and laid a shaky hand on her back. "No. She's not breathing."

"You did good, sweetie." I held out my hand and helped him up. "No. She's not breathing. She—" I swallowed. Hard. "She's been stabbed in the neck. And there's a lot of blood."

"Deputies and emergency personnel are on their way, ma'am. Again, please stay on the phone with me."

"All right. We'll go downstairs and wait for them." I beckoned to PJ, miming that we should be careful leaving the room. We both did our best to avoid stepping on the stuff scattered over the carpet, but a lot of that damage had already been done.

Once we were in the hallway, PJ grabbed my hand. "Ohmygod, ohmygod, ohmygod. I never *really* wanted to be in a horror movie." He started to laugh a little wildly. "Although if I were writing one, I'd probably have picked Ava for the first victim." He clapped a hand over his mouth, but must have remembered where that hand had been, because he snatched it away and held it away from himself as if it was contaminated. "I don't mean to be disrespectful, Tash, but this is just so... so *typical* of Ava."

He stood aside and let me walk downstairs first. When I reached the vestibule I turned left to flick on the porch light as PJ stumbled down behind me.

"*Augh!*"

I whirled at his cry, my heel skidding on the marble tiles. PJ was backed against the wall. Facing him on top of Ava's foyer table was the cat, her paw hooked in PJ's boa.

"I've seen this on *Crime Scene Investigation*," PJ wailed. "The po-po's going to think the cat is fingering me for the crime!"

"I don't think feline testimony is admissible in court." Reaction was setting in for me too. My fingers shook, making it tough to work my glove back on, especially while sandwiching my phone between my shoulder and cheek. My dress no longer felt like it was hugging me—now it was squeezing the breath out of me like a satin anaconda.

PJ stared, wide-eyed, at his feline accuser. "It could happen." He tugged the boa away from the cat, leaving a tuft of teal feathers on her claws. "They've accepted identification from dogs before."

Sirens began wailing in the distance. I opened the door and peered out into the night. "I'm pretty sure those were trained tracking dogs or K-9 units."

"Pardon me if I don't want to be part of the landmark case where a cat becomes the star witness." He raised his hands as if to cover his face, but stopped, staring down at them bleakly. "This is worse than flu season. I need to wash my hands."

"Powder room's right there." PJ scuttled in as I tried to regulate my breathing. *Calm. Calm. I can do this.*

"Ma'am? Ma'am, are you still there?"

I startled, nearly dropping the phone. I'd almost forgotten the 9-1-1 operator was still on the line. I swallowed hard. "Yes. Yes, I'm here."

"Where are you right now?"

"I'm downstairs in Ava's foyer. My friend is in the bathroom. Once he comes out, we'll sit in the living room and wait for help to arrive." My voice was shaking worse than my hands.

PJ returned to the foyer and shot me a forlorn look. "I'm sorry. I just can't get my head around this. The only things I seem capable of are inappropriate comments alternating with bouts of hysteria."

Careful to keep my phone clear of PJ's feathers and vintage suit, I wrapped him in a hug. He returned it, his hands still a little damp against my back. For a minute, we just stood there in the middle of the vestibule, with the cat eyeing the fluttering ends of PJ's boa and the sirens getting louder and louder.

"Is it wrong," PJ murmured with a light hiccup, "that all I can think of besides inappropriate jokes is how absolutely, bone-deep grateful I am that it was Ava and not you?"

I leaned back a little so I could look down into his eyes. "Why would it have been me? We don't even know what caused her death."

He glared at me. "How many pairs of scissors do you own, LaTashia? How many staple guns? How many noxious liquids?" He pointed an unsteady finger up the stairs as red and blue flashed through the sidelights of Ava's front door. "Crafting is *dangerous*! I mean the paper cuts *alone*—"

There was a knock on the half-open door. "Ms. Van Buren?"

We both turned at the sound of the deep voice, although we didn't release each other, not yet. "Yes, that's me."

"Dear sweet heaven," PJ murmured. "He looks just like John Cho."

PJ had a point—the navy-suited man in the doorway looked very much like the actor—the craggier, edgier Cho from *Sleepy Hollow*, not the smoother Sulu version. He was flanked by a woman with a salt-and-pepper bob whose pantsuit was the female version of his.

"I'm Detective Bae and this is my partner, Detective Huber." Both of them flashed their badges.

"Bae?" PJ muttered. "Seriously?"

Either Detective Bae didn't hear PJ or he chose to ignore him. "Perhaps you could step out here and allow the emergency team to get to work?"

"Of course." I had to tug on PJ's arm to get him to move because he was still staring at Detective Bae. The two detectives stood aside to let us exit onto the porch. "Hello?" I said into the phone. "The police have arrived."

"Thank you, ma'am. They'll take things from here."

Detective Bae waited for me to stow my phone in my purse. "Where's the victim?"

I grabbed PJ's hand. *Victim.* Clearly Ava was dead, and probably not of natural causes given the die embedded in her throat. But *victim*? If PJ was right, and she'd been done in by her crafting tools, I'd never look at my Cuttlebug the same way. "Upstairs," I croaked. "First door on the left. In the closet."

The EMTs paused on the porch steps with their equipment, and as Detective Huber gave them low-voiced instructions, a fluffy blur shot out the door and dove into the hydrangea bush.

Detective Bae startled. "What the…"

"Cat." Detective Huber raised an eyebrow at me. "Correct?"

"Yes. That's right. It's Ava's cat."

"Ava. That's the victim?"

"Y-yes." I swallowed against a lump in my throat. "Ava Cornell. This is her house."

Detective Huber nodded and disappeared inside with the EMTs.

"Tash." PJ grabbed my arm. "They're putting up *crime scene* tape."

Detective Bae transferred his attention from me to PJ. It might have been the shadows cast by the harsh porch light and the red-blue flashes from yet another emergency vehicle that pulled up in Ava's driveway, but I could swear Detective Bae jerked, eyes widening, as he took in PJ from fedora to polished black wingtips.

And of course, the boa.

Bae cleared his throat. "You are?"

"PJ Purdy."

"And what does PJ stand for?"

PJ slid a glance at me as if to say *wait for it.* "Peter Johnson." Sure enough, Bae blinked and his rather austere mouth twitched. PJ huffed and shoved his glasses up with a knuckle. "Look, my mother's maiden name was Johnson, she was a giant *Spiderman* nerd, and was completely oblivious that she'd doomed me to a lifetime of sexual innuendo, okay? At least my last name isn't Richards."

Bae rubbed a hand across his jaw. "I didn't say anything."

PJ glared at him. "You were thinking it. I could tell."

Bae didn't answer, but that might have been because the two people who'd been taping off Ava's yard and driveway approached him. He turned away to discuss something with them, too low-voiced for us to hear.

PJ tugged on my arm, drawing me a little farther down the porch. "I can't believe it. Not only is there *crime scene* tape, but Detective Hottie is totally judging me. Do you think it's because of my name?"

I raised an eyebrow. "Didn't you do the same with him? I mean, *Detective Hottie*?"

"That's different! I mean if you look like him and your name is *Bae*, you're just begging for it." But although PJ's tone was tart, from the way his boa was shimmying, he was trembling. I could relate—I still felt off balance myself, and it wasn't because of my stilettos.

Detective Huber emerged from the house as the two new personnel donned those white hazmat-looking suits. One of them handed a couple of plastic bags to her and then they picked up their kits and disappeared inside.

Huber approached us and handed us each a bag. "If you could please remove your shoes and place them in here?"

I glanced down at my best heels. "Our shoes?"

"Yes. You were at the death scene when you made the 9-1-1 call, correct?"

"*Death scene*?" PJ clutched my arm. "We didn't see her die."

Huber regarded PJ somberly. "We refer to any crime scene with a dead body as a death scene."

"Wait a minute. Are you *homicide* detectives?" PJ's voice squeaked on *homicide*. When Huber nodded, his grip tightened. "Oh my god, Tash, we're *suspects*!"

CHAPTER ELEVEN

Suspects. Were we? I didn't have PJ's encyclopedic knowledge of *Forensic Files* and every single *CSI* series, but I suppose it made sense—first on the scene and all that.

Detective Huber should play professional poker, because although her expression wasn't unkind, she definitely wasn't giving anything away. "Nobody is a suspect yet. We treat any death scene as a potential homicide until proven otherwise or we risk missing critical evidence."

"I *warned* you, Tash." PJ's whisper wasn't as quiet as he probably imagined. "The person who makes the 9-1-1 call is *always* in the cross-hairs. It *never* fails."

This time, both Huber's eyebrows rose. "Let me guess. *Forensic Files* fan?" PJ nodded. "Then you should know that forensics doesn't just identify the guilty, it also clears the innocent." She gestured to a uniformed deputy who was standing on the lawn as motionless as Ava's collection of garden gnomes. "After we bag your shoes, Deputy Ramirez will stay with you here on the porch and keep you company until Bae and I are done touring the scene."

"I can't believe this," PJ moaned as he untied his shoelaces. "Even if we're not technically suspects, my dreams of being a *person of interest* involve meeting my soulmate across a crowded dance floor. And while handcuffs might have been involved at some point, they were always the *fun* kind, lined with lambs-wool or tasteful pink fur."

As I slipped off my heels and dropped them into the bag, flakes of crushed crystal fell off the soles. My stomach roiled. We had stomped all over that *death scene*. What evidence had we already destroyed?

Huber handed us both a pair of blue paper booties. PJ held his up, pinched between his thumb and forefinger. "These are so not my color." He slipped them on over his teal and purple argyle socks. "I hope Ava's lawn service has kept the thistles and blackberry brambles under control, otherwise the walk to your car is going to be murder." He jerked his chin up, eyes wide as he stared at Huber. "I mean *painful*. Not murder. Because murder wouldn't be anything to joke about. Even if that's what happened. Which it might not have. Happened." He scrubbed his hands over his face. "God, just shoot me now." He winced. "Not that anyone should shoot anyone. Definitely not me. I don't want to shoot. Be shot. Do the shooting. Can we go now?"

Huber shook her head. "We'll want to take statements from both of you separately. If you'll join Deputy Ramirez now, I hope we won't keep you waiting long."

I padded a few steps across Ava's porch, PJ right behind me. The rough boards pricked my bare feet through the thin blue booties—the whole deck was in need of a light sanding and a fresh coat of paint. *Why am I thinking of that now?* Deputy Ramirez gestured to one of Ava's bright yellow Adirondack chairs in an invitation to be seated.

I eyed its tilted back and *very* short legs. "If I sit there, do you promise to help me up again? Once I get *that* low, in *this* dress? No way will I be escaping under my own steam."

Ramirez managed to remain stoic for about three seconds before the corners of his mouth twitched and then broadened into a wide grin. That, combined with his uniform, reminded me of Ponch from *CHiPs* and I couldn't help return the smile.

So sue me—PJ has his cinematic catnip and I have mine.

"You can count on me, ma'am." He held out his hand to help me lower myself into the chair. "I'm here to protect and serve."

Once I was settled, he motioned for PJ to sit on the swing at the other end of the porch several feet away. PJ's jaw sagged, and he exchanged a wide-eyed glance with me. He mouthed *suspects*. "Can't we sit together? There are two chairs."

"Sorry. Not until after the detectives have a chance to question you."

PJ sighed, but trudged over and plopped down. The swing was high enough that his bootied toes barely touched the porch, and his boa fluttered in the breeze as the swing gently swayed. *Why didn't Ramirez offer me that seat? At least it has cushions and an even chance that my hips wouldn't be level with my ankles.*

I revised my opinion of his cuteness as I rubbed my arms where the gooseflesh had risen again. This time, though, it was from the chilly air and not from the shock of discovering Ava's body.

At least I didn't think so, but shock was a funny thing.

I huddled in my chair with PJ casting forlorn looks at me every few minutes until Bae and Huber emerged from Ava's house. I expected them to split up, one of them taking PJ's statement and the other taking mine, but they both headed for me first.

Huber was wearing her poker face again, but Bae might have been carved from granite. I struggled to sit forward and as promised, Ramirez offered me a hand. Bae glanced at PJ, then motioned for me to follow them down the steps to the front lawn where the coolness of the grass through the thin bootie soles chilled me as though it were November instead of June . Even without shoes on, I had a couple of inches on Bae and a couple more on Huber, but that didn't make either of them less intimidating.

"She's dead, isn't she? I mean, it was pretty obvious, but it's true?" At Huber's nod, I pressed my hands against my cheeks. "What happened? How did she die?"

"That's for the coroner to determine," Bae said severely. "She's okayed the EMTs to transport the body to the morgue, but she won't have a report until she conducts her examination." He stared pointedly at my hands. "Tell me, Ms. Van Buren, is it normal for you to wear gloves while visiting your acquaintances?"

I frowned at the accusation in his tone. "They're *cocktail* gloves. PJ and I were on our way to Martini Blues."

"And you always wear gloves for cocktails?"

"Back down, Cameron," Huber said. "It's not that unusual. Not for that venue."

He faced her, his mouth turned down. "Are you telling me you wear gloves when you head out for a beer?"

"No, but my wife does." She shrugged at his disbelieving expression. "It's a thing." She nudged him with her elbow and something that was almost a smirk flickered across her face. "Why don't you go take Mr. Purdy's statement. I'll chat with Ms. Van Buren."

He narrowed his eyes. "Sarah..."

His voice held a definite note of warning, but it didn't faze Huber. She met his stare calmly. "Unless you want *me* to take Mr. Purdy's statement." She checked her watch. "Make up your mind, Cam. We've got an investigation to run."

Detective Bae glared at his partner, then rubbed the back of his neck, muttering something under his breath. But he stalked up the porch steps and over to PJ. When PJ tried to stand, the swing belled out behind him, causing him to stumble, catapulting him onto Bae's chest. Bae caught him by the shoulders and steadied him, then dropped his hands. Fedora askew, PJ tossed his boa over his shoulder and lifted his chin. Oh lord, did Bae intend to intimidate him? PJ was already so agitated...

"Ms. Van Buren?"

Huber's quiet voice called my attention away from PJ's standoff with Detective Hottie. "I'm sorry. What was that?"

"What was your relationship to the deceased?"

Deceased. My knees wobbled, and I took a wider stance to steady myself. *Ava is deceased.* "Oh god. Her daughter. I have to call her daughter."

"Easy there." Huber took my elbow and walked me over to a garden bench flanked by two gnomes. "Please have a seat. We'll contact her next of kin."

I bit my lip. If I were the one who'd lost a loved one, I'd want the news broken to me by somebody I knew. Somebody who cared. "But—"

"Until we know more about what happened here, you need to leave such communication to the police."

I needed to tell Pops, too. That wouldn't be an easy conversation. "But—"

"I'm afraid I really must insist. You can't discuss this case with anybody unless you want to risk interfering with an ongoing investigation."

I stared up at her. She and Bae were playing things close to their chests, but they must have some idea by now whether Ava's death was an accident. Although how likely was it that she trashed her own craft room, jammed a die into her own throat, and collapsed in her closet—*closing the door behind her*? But who would want to murder Ava?

I had to cover my mouth to hide an inappropriate laugh because I could almost hear PJ's voice in my head: *"You mean besides everybody who knew her?"* But then the EMTs emerged from the house with a black body bag on a stretcher and I lost all desire to laugh.

In fact, I was afraid I might throw up.

"Ms. Van Buren, I know this is difficult, but the sooner we can get through your statement, the sooner we can let you go."

I nodded, but couldn't take my eyes off that body bag as the EMTs loaded it—*her*—into the ambulance.

She beckoned to Ramirez, who trotted down the porch steps to join us. "The deputy will be recording your responses. Please state your full name and address."

"LaTashia Danielle Fredericka Van Buren." I had to give her props—she didn't even blink at my mile-long moniker. I gave her my address. "But please call me Tash."

"Very well, Tash. What was your relationship to Ava Cornell?"

"We're—we *were* friends of a sort, although my grandfather was the one with the real connection. After her husband passed, Pops asked me to reach out to her, and she joined one of my crafting circles."

"What kind of crafts?"

"Scrapbooking and paper crafts, mostly. I belong to others, but paper crafting was Ava's primary interest."

"When did you last see Ms. Cornell alive?"

"Sunday at about 3:30 p.m." The ambulance glided away, siren silent and lights doused. *No need to hurry anymore. She's gone.* "She attended a class I taught at Central Paper and Supply. A Christmas card class."

"Did she seem in good spirits?"

"Yes. Well, good for her."

"She was a difficult person?"

I took a deep breath, my grandmother's strict rule about not speaking ill of the dead warring with the need not to interfere with the investigation. "She could be. Before she retired, she was a critical care nurse. Her patients, including my grandfather, appreciated her although her coworkers were less than complimentary. She didn't suffer fools gladly, and she wasn't fussy about who she considered foolish."

"I see."

"After her retirement, with her husband gone and her daughter living up in Seattle, she became a bit of a curmudgeon. Demanding."

"Do you think she made enemies as a result?"

I wrinkled my nose. "Some? Although I'd call them non-friends as opposed to enemies per se."

"Can you think of anyone who might wish her harm?"

PJ's mental commentary again: *Other than everybody?* But he didn't mean that any more than I did. "Not bodily harm, no. Nothing more than serious annoyance when she snapped a rare die out from under their nose or criticized their taste in alcohol inks."

Huber glanced at the porch where the crime scene techs were peeling out of their protective gear. "Why were you here this evening?"

"Ava left her basic kit at the store after the class on Sunday. I intended to return it to her after our regular meeting earlier this evening, but she didn't show up."

"Was that unusual?"

"Very. But she wasn't answerable to any of us. The scrapbooking circle meetings aren't mandatory—they're just a chance for us to work together on projects of our choice. We hold the meetings at the store so we have ready access to any supplies we might need."

"What made you decide to stop by?" She gestured to my outfit. "Clearly you and Mr. Purdy had other plans."

"I was a little worried. Plus, crafters are quite attached to our own kits." I lifted my palms in a shrug. "We get them arranged just how we like them so being without them—"

"I understand. My wife is a quilter, and the gods help anybody who comes between her and her sewing basket."

I smiled shakily. "So you get it. Good." I watched the techs pack up. Their expressions didn't give anything away either. "Since Ava's house—this place—isn't too far out of the way, I convinced PJ to stop by here and return the kit." I peered through the gloom at PJ, who was looking decidedly mulish in his interview with Bae.

"Did he take much convincing?"

"Hmmm? Oh. No. He's just a very creative complainer."

The techs headed toward their van. One of them gestured to Bae, who left PJ on the porch in order to confer with her. PJ gave me a goggle-eyed stare and mouthed *oh my god*.

Bae nodded to Huber, and she looked down at me. "I'd like you to walk me through what happened between your arrival and the 9-1-1 call. Do you feel up to that?"

Since I didn't have socks, I settled for pulling up my gloves. "As I'll ever be."

CHAPTER TWELVE

Let me tell you something. Those hazmat suits or whatever they call them? *Not* meant for slipping on over a cocktail dress. But I finally wrestled myself into the thing, and the five of us— Deputy Ramirez joined the two detectives—headed onto the porch.

Detective Bae stopped us at the door and turned to me. "So the house was dark when you arrived. What did you do then?"

"Since I know where Ava keeps—*kept* her key, we decided to drop the kit inside. I've done the same before."

"'She made a habit of forgetting her kit?"

"Not the kit, but other things. Supplies or tools that she asked me to pick up for her."

"How many times would you say you've been here?"

I gnawed on my lip. "Maybe… a dozen?"

Bae turned to PJ. "What about you?"

PJ blinked. "Me? *I've* never been here before. Ava was Tash's probl—er, friend."

Bae made a noncommittal sound. "To your knowledge, Ms. Van Buren, did anyone else know where she kept the house key?"

"Well, her daughter, of course. Probably the rest of the scrapbooking circle, since she told me about it in the middle of a session. There could be more, of course. I didn't know any of her other friends."

"Assuming she had any," PJ muttered.

Bae shot PJ a sharp glance. "Could you point out where you found the key?"

"Up there." I pointed to the jutting trim. "But we didn't need to use it. The door was ajar."

"Did you find that odd?"

"Not really. Ava wasn't particularly good at closing doors."

"She expected other people to do it for her," PJ said.

Bae fixed PJ with a bland stare. "People such as you?"

"People such as *anybody*. She wasn't picky, as long as she didn't have to do it herself."

Bae's eyes narrowed slightly, but he didn't respond. I tried to give PJ a wordless *TMI* warning. It seemed to work, because he clamped his lips shut and suddenly got very interested in the hydrangeas.

Huber gestured to the open door. "So you noticed the door was ajar. Then what?"

"I pushed it open and called for Ava, but there was no answer. So we went inside."

"Why not just set the kit inside and leave?"

PJ snorted although he was still communing with the bushes.

"Do you have something to add, Mr. Purdy?" Huber asked.

He quickly tucked his boa inside his hazmat suit. "Not a thing."

"What PJ means," I said quickly, "is that Ava had definite ideas about where her craft supplies should live, and that didn't include inside her front door. Since we were already there, dropping it in her craft room made the most sense."

PJ nodded sagely. "It was self-defense."

Bae's attention sharpened. "Self-defense?"

"If we left the silly thing for *her* to carry upstairs herself, Tash would never have heard the end of it."

I glared at PJ. He'd been beside himself to think we were suspects, but now he seemed determined to make us sound as *suspicious* as possible. "*Anyway*, we decided to take the kit to the craft room. When we got upstairs—"

"Oh. Oh!" PJ shook his boa, and the fluff flew as usual. "Don't forget the alien attack."

Huber seemed mesmerized by a tiny feather caught on Bae's left eyebrow, but she didn't point it out. "Alien attack?"

"He means the cat. It raced downstairs as we were heading up and nearly knocked PJ tail over tin cup."

"Please." He sniffed. "My reflexes are *excellent*. I was totally in control."

"Yes. Well." Bae cleared his throat. "Mr. Purdy, I'd like you to stay down here with Deputy Ramirez. Ms. Van Buren, if you'll follow me."

It was probably just as well PJ wasn't part of our little parade up the stairs, since he seemed to be bent on incriminating us. Huber touched my elbow before I mounted the first step.

"Be careful of the handrails. They've been dusted for fingerprints and you don't want to get the residue on your gloves."

I peered down at the banisters and I couldn't help it—part of my brain went *there* and I thought *If Ava sees that crap all over her house, she's gonna die.* So by the time I joined Bae outside the craft room door, I was sniffling a little.

The floor was dotted with those little numbered plastic tents, marking where the crime scene team had found some kind of evidence. *So many.* I tried not to look at the closet door.

"Ms. Van Buren." Bae's voice was quiet, as if he didn't want his words to drift downstairs where PJ was apparently giving Deputy Ramirez fashion advice. "You and Mr. Purdy intended to visit the cocktail lounge this evening, correct?"

"Yes. Martini Blues. It's one of our favorite places to decompress."

"Why did you require, er, decompression?"

"Well, we'd had a stressful couple of days, and I have to admit that Ava was part of that stress." I told them about the craft show and the class. "So we were more than ready for a little reward."

"Did you get ready for your outing at the same time and place?"

"No. I had the scrapbooking meet-up, so I took my outfit with me and changed in the store's restroom. When PJ came to meet me, he was already dressed for the club."

"Including the, er, unusual neckwear?" Huber's gaze flicked to that errant feather and coughed into her hand. Bae frowned at her, which made the feather flutter.

"Yes. He bought it at the show on Saturday. He's quite fond of it."

"Helloooo?" PJ called from downstairs. "Do you need me to come up there yet?"

"No." Bae's voice cracked, making the word come out in an odd couple of syllables. He cleared his throat. "No. You're fine, er, I mean, you can stay where you are." He caught Huber's gaze. "What?"

"Nothing," she murmured. "Tash, could you point out the item that you and Mr. Purdy brought into the house?"

"Yes. That bag next to the closet." I pointed at the kit, then peered at it more closely. "Wait a moment. I think that might be mine."

"You brought your own possessions into Ms. Cornell's home?" Bae had recovered his granite-faced composure.

"Not on purpose. My bag and Ava's are identical. She purchased hers because she liked mine. I've had mine longer, but hers has a little splotch there near the handle"—I pointed— "from when Ava dropped a brush loaded with acrylic paint, then promptly blamed me for the accident." I rolled my eyes. Ava had claimed I bumped her, but in truth she was so busy critiquing poor Nikki, instead of minding her own project, that she'd missed the table. "PJ must have grabbed the wrong one."

"Hmmm." Bae threaded his way through the evidence markers and hunkered down next to the kit. "Can you describe what's in it?"

Let's see…" I pictured the contents in my mind and counted off on my fingers. "My favorite paper-cutting scissors, another pair for cutting ribbon, various adhesives, cosmetic sponges for blending, paint brushes, Copic markers, alcohol inks, a work station mat, acid free pens for journaling, a ruler—" *Oops. Ran out of fingers.* I dropped my hands to my sides. "A paper cutter, an Exacto knife, tweezers, a cloth to wipe fingerprints off of photographs, an apron… You know, just the basics."

Bae blinked, his eyes a bit glassy. "All that is, er, basic?"

"Of course. Oh! There's a stitched label with my name and address on the back pocket. I got those fabric labels made for next to nothing to hand-sew on all my bags and aprons."

Bae checked the pocket and nodded sharply. "Yes, it's yours."

I held out my hand. "Could I have it back, please?"

"I'm sorry." He stood up. "We'll have to keep this as evidence for the time being."

"But it wasn't even here when Ava— When she—" I swallowed, my stomach suddenly turning over. *When Ava died.*

Huber gripped my elbow as I wobbled. "Doing all right?" I pressed one gloved hand to my mouth and nodded. "Once the investigation is over, we'll be sure you get it back."

"Thank you," I croaked.

Bae dodged a small mound of glitter and crushed crystals on his way over to us. "That will be all for now. The two of you are free to go. We'll be in touch if we need anything further."

I tottered down the stairs with Huber at my heels. PJ rushed over to me once I made it to the bottom. "Tash, sweetie, are you okay?"

"Mostly. But I don't think I can face cocktails tonight."

"God, me neither. But I could definitely use a stiff drink."

"Likewise. And I *do* have a bottle of gin, tonic, and some limes at my apartment."

He made grabby hands. "Take me to it."

"You'll have to leave the boa in your car, though. I don't want teal feathers all over my apartment."

He lifted his chin with a pretty good approximation of his usual attitude, but he was still paler than normal. "Really, LaTashia. You above anyone should be willing to sacrifice convenience for style. But I shall bear up manfully under the adversity. What should we— *Ack!*" PJ staggered back as the cat shot across his blue booties. "Drat that animal. It's going to *kill* me." Pink suffused his face, and he glanced at Huber, who was still standing at the foot of the stairs with her poker face firmly in place. "Not in a, you know, *fatal* way. I mean, I'm sure the cat isn't *homicidal*, at least no more than most cats, although considering she belonged to Ava—" He covered his face with both hands. "I'll just stop talking now, shall I?"

"You can try," I said, but knowing PJ as I did, I considered it highly unlikely.

Sure enough, he dropped his hands and whirled to where the cat had taken up the same spot on the table. "Oh my god, Tash. The cat. We can't just abandon it here. It'll *die*."

I patted PJ's back. "Maybe Ava's daughter will want it."

"But she's not here now. I'm sure the cat has *needs*. We can't leave it in the house where its kitty-mama... well... you know."

I cut a glance at the staircase where Bae had finally made an appearance—with the feather still stuck to his eyebrow. I wasn't sure how aware cats were of human mortality, but PJ was right —it would be cruel to leave it here with no caretaker.

Bae cleared his throat again, something he seemed to do a lot. "We'll contact animal control. They'll take it into custody."

"Custody?" PJ's indignant tone held a hint of outrage. "You're *arresting* her?"

"Of course not. But we don't know when the house will be released as a crime scene. We can't risk the cat compromising the evidence, and as you pointed out—"

"Evidence?" PJ's eyes narrowed. "Is *that* all you're worried about? She's a living, breathing—"

"I was about to say," Bae cut in with a glare, "that we don't want it to suffer for lack of care."

"Well." PJ crossed his arms. "All right then. But you are *not* allowed to *arrest* her."

"Animal control isn't—"

"It's okay," I said, before PJ and Bae could get into a wrestling match over appropriate cat husbandry. "The executive director of the local cat foster care organization belongs to my mixed media and collage meet-up. I can give her a call."

PJ rolled his eyes. "Why am I not surprised?" He leaned over and whispered to Huber out of the corner of his mouth. "Tash is like the Kevin Bacon of Portland crafting."

CHAPTER THIRTEEN

"Kevin Bacon?" Bae's brows drew together. "What does he have to do with anything?"

Huber's lips twitched. "It's a thing, Cam. Kevin Bacon is supposedly the center of the Hollywood universe—no actor is any farther than six steps away from him in movie terms."

"Exactly!" PJ punctuated the word with a jab of his finger into Bae's biceps, but then shook out his hand as if he'd injured it. "And I'm convinced Tash is the center of anything crafting in Portland, and for some reason, everyone in Portland is connected to somebody who does crafts." He turned to Huber. "I bet she knows someone who knows your quilter wife."

"Fiber arts and paper crafts are really two different spheres," I murmured, my face heating.

PJ held up a palm. "Please, LaTashia. Your humility is admirable, but I'm convinced that I'm right. If not someone, then someone who knows someone who knows someone who —"

"That'll do, PJ." I looked at the cat and bit my lip. "I'm not sure my friend can collect the cat before tomorrow, though. You'll have to take it overnight."

"Me?" His eyes widened. "Why not you? You're the one with the connection."

"Yes, but I'm allergic. *Highly* allergic. I've been teetering on the edge of a sneezing fit since we walked through the door."

He huffed out a breath. "Of course you are. Fine." He glared at Bae. "May we please take *custody* of the cat?"

Huber shared a glance with her partner, and although I couldn't detect any obvious communication, she nodded. "Yes. Although why does the cat have a mouthful of teal feathers?"

"Oh." PJ flipped the end of his boa, which drew the cat's laser-eyed stare. "She apparently mistook it for a bird. Or else she has a highly developed fashion sense."

"We'll need the cat carrier."

PJ squinted up at me. "How do you know she *has* a carrier?"

"Vets require cats to be in a carrier for office visits."

He smirked. "I suppose you know this because there's a vet in one of your many crafting groups?"

I hiked my purse strap further up my shoulder. "No."

"No? Are you *suuuurrre?*"

I glanced sidelong at Bae. What would he think of PJ's playfulness in the face of Ava's death? Would he think PJ was callous—or worse, *guilty*? "Yes. But Evy's son-in-law is a vet."

"Ah *ha!* I knew it."

I sighed and turned to Huber. "Is it all right if we check the garage for the carrier?"

"Why would it be there?" PJ asked.

"It's only logical. If you're taking the cat somewhere in the car—like to the vet—you don't want to dig through some closet upstairs to find the carrier."

"Good point. Let us *investigate.*" He looked at Bae. "If you don't mind."

"Sarah. Go with them."

Huber shook her head, but in resignation rather than denial apparently, because she gestured for me to take the lead. I headed into the kitchen and through the laundry room where the door to the garage was located. Sure enough, the cat carrier was on a shelf in front of Ava's Buick land boat. I handed it to PJ.

He clutched the handle, then blinked up at me. "Wait. I don't have any kitty accoutrements at my place. She'll need food. Dishes. Catnip mice."

I spotted a telltale green bag next to the single concrete step. "Kitty litter is probably more to the point than catnip mice."

PJ wrinkled his nose. "Eww."

Huber grabbed the bag with a definite smirk. "I'll tell Cam to look for the litter pan."

PJ watched her retreat into the laundry room. "I think I like her."

I just sighed. "Come on. Let's find the cat food."

We managed to get everything except the cat carrier—and the cat—loaded into the back of Moocher, with Bae looking downright sour after emptying the litter pan.

"Now comes the hard part," I said. "Getting the cat into the carrier."

"Don't they go in automatically?" PJ flung the end of his boa over his shoulder, hitting Bae in the jaw—which at least dislodged the feather in his eyebrow, although it deposited three more in his hair. "I thought cats loved empty boxes."

"Not this kind. Too many unpleasant associations. Come on." I had to stiffen my spine to walk back into the house when Ava would never have the chance again. It didn't help that every step—the marble tiles, the stone pavers, the wooden decking—was *hyperbolized* by the thin booties.

The cat was still sitting on the table, one hind paw lifted as she cleaned between her claws.

"Good grief," PJ muttered. "She must be related to Freddy Krueger." He set the carrier on the floor in front of the table and opened its wire door. "Here, kitty, kitty, kitty. Go into the nice box so we can get you out of the murder house." He winced. "I mean, so you can go on a nice visit to Uncle PJ's apartment."

The cat was unimpressed by the suggestion and continued her foot bath. "You're going to have to pick her up, Peej." My nose was already twitching with the need to sneeze. "The sooner the better."

"Oh, *fine*." He approached her gingerly, and she stopped licking her paw to stare, unblinking, at PJ's boa. He edged closer and grabbed her behind the front legs. She went limp in his hands. "Hey. This isn't so hard."

But as soon as he got her close to the carrier, she exploded into action, squirming and yowling.

PJ, to his credit, didn't drop her. "Oh my god, she *is* an alien! She's sprouted at least eight more legs. Ow!" A long bloody gash opened on the back of his hand, although I hadn't seen the blow.

"I've got an idea." I slid over to him on the slick marble tiles and unwound the boa from his neck. I shook it in the cat's face once, then tossed it into the carrier. She planted her rear feet on PJ's chest and launched herself onto the floor, then zipped inside. I clanged the door shut and latched it. "There. Piece of cake. Now let's get out of here."

I didn't have to ask PJ twice. He practically leaped behind Moocher's wheel, leaving me to listen to Bae reiterate his ominous *We'll be in touch* when he handed me his and Huber's cards. I made a mental note to call Huber in the morning to find out if they'd contacted Ava's daughter, Rebecca. Even if we weren't allowed to discuss the case with anyone not involved, I wanted to send her a note offering my condolences and ask if I could do anything to help.

As soon as I was belted in, PJ pulled away from the curb. "Thank goodness. I thought we'd *never* escape." In the back seat, the cat let out the weirdest yowl. PJ glanced over his shoulder, his eyes wide. "Holy crap, Tash. It sounds like she's saying *Ava*."

A shiver climbed up my spine. "That's impossible."

"If we were in—"

"A horror movie, yes, I know. But we've got our own horror to deal with now. We don't need to *borrow* any from your favorite obsession."

He sighed and gripped the wheel harder. "I know. And I just realized we can't get sloshed over at your place. Even if we didn't have work tomorrow—and Vinh has me scheduled to provision *two* new servers—we can't exactly leave the cat in the car." When I sneezed, he shot me a wry half smile. "And we can't take her inside your place either."

I pulled my lace-edged handkerchief out of my purse and blotted my watering eyes. "That's for sure."

PJ braked for a red light and leaned his forehead against the steering wheel. "Why couldn't I shut up back there? I mean, I *know* it was a shock finding Ava like… like *that*—"

"You think?"

"But every word out of my mouth was as good as a confession. You'd think I'd never seen an episode of *Criminal Minds* in my *life*! And did you see the way Detective Hottie kept giving us the side-eye? He *definitely* thinks we did it."

I sighed. "It's been a long and *very* stressful day. Let's not make things worse. I know we can't indulge in gin and tonics, but…" I pointed out the window at a Burgerville.

"Fresh strawberry milkshakes! Yes!"

They weren't martinis, but after the day we'd had, they were almost as good.

CHAPTER FOURTEEN

It was a good thing that PJ and I decided to forgo the alcohol last night, because the next day at work wasn't anything I could have faced with a hangover. As it was, everything had a vaguely unfocused quality, as if my mental eyes needed glasses. I'd experienced that before, so I knew exactly what the cause was.

I'd lost a friend.

While I might get involved in answering emails or polishing my product launch presentation, momentarily forgetting what had happened, I'd suddenly flash on Ava lying facedown in her closet and things would go blurry again. Then I'd feel guilty for not feeling worse. Yes, Ava's death was a shock and a sorrow, but it didn't completely debilitate me. She hadn't been family or even a particularly close friend. If, heaven forbid, something had happened to PJ, I wouldn't be able to function with even a *hint* of normalcy. As it was, Neal didn't notice anything at all when he popped into my office just as I'd finished the final numbers for my launch forecast. Either I was better at hiding my feelings than PJ claimed, or else Neal chalked it up to the usual aftermath of customer drama.

With a *tink, tink, tink* he knocked on my metal door frame to announce his entrance. "Good morning, Tash." He glanced at my monitor. "Sorry to interrupt you while you're neck deep in a spreadsheet, but I need to borrow you for a minute or two."

Right. A minute or two. I resigned myself to Neal's usual half hour of sidling up to his point. I saved my work and swiveled my chair to face him. He didn't sit down, which was... ominous. Instead, he rocked on his heels and alternated finger snaps with driving his right fist into his left palm—a sure sign he was about to ask me to do something that wasn't remotely connected to my job.

"What can I do for you, Neal?"

Snap snap punch. Snap snap punch. "The thing is, Tash, morale is down." I made a noncommittal noise. "We need to raise everyone's spirits. Fire people—"

"*Fire* people?" The hairs on my neck lifted. "How do layoffs boost morale?"

Neal laughed a little too long. "You're such a kidder, Tash. Fire people *up*. Get 'em excited."

"Excited about what?"

"About their jobs. About the company. You know, put the *fun* in *functional*." He beamed at me, clearly waiting for a response.

I had nothin'. I just blinked at him.

"Right." *Snap snap punch.* "Excellent. Glad we're on the same page. Give me your recommendations by... shall we say... end of the week?"

Maybe I was still disoriented by Ava's death, but Neal was making even less sense than usual. "Recommendations about *what*?"

"Morale boosters, Tash. Excitement builders. Fun!"

I took a steadying breath. "Neal, you do realize that I'm in the middle of a major project launch and that our biggest trade show is only two months away?"

"So? It's not like this is *work*. You do this kind of stuff all the time."

"Neal—"

"Just think about it. I'm sure you'll have a dozen ideas before lunchtime." He bared his teeth in his used-car-salesman smile. "Then all you'll have to do is put 'em in motion."

I smoothed my donut-print skirt over my knees—it was the only thing keeping me from throttling my boss. "Neal, I don't think—"

"Whoa." Neal widened his eyes at my exposed-gear wall clock in obviously manufactured surprise. "Is that the time? Got a lunch meeting with the executive team. Gotta go."

He was gone before I could get another word out. *Wait until PJ hears about this one.*

Oh, goodness. PJ.

Between this morning's spreadsheet marathon and Neal's unwanted visit, I hadn't had a minute to check in on him. He was probably experiencing the same disorientation that I was—he'd discovered Ava, after all.

Neal was right about one thing—it was almost lunchtime. PJ had mentioned the big server project today, but surely Vinh would let him take a lunch break. I'd insist if I had to—PJ's boss had a tendency to treat his team as though they were still students during finals week, doing all-nighters to finish up projects and subsisting on coffee and vending machine junk food.

At least I can take one thing off his plate. I pulled out my personal cell phone and looked up the contact for my friend who was the executive director of the local cat rescue league. As I was about to connect, my phone buzzed with an incoming call, the screen displaying the fluffy bunny picture I'd assigned to Nikki. "Hey, Nikki."

"Hi, Tash. It's Nik— Oh, you already know that."

"Yup. Caller ID. It's a thing. What can I do for—" My throat thickened and things went cattywampus again. *She doesn't know.* But I didn't want to deliver the news about Ava over the phone. Besides, the detectives had warned PJ and me not to discuss the case with anyone. Although there was no way timid little Nikki could possibly be a suspect, I didn't want to risk Bae's ire—or a possible charge of interfering with an investigation. I cleared my throat and tried to sound normal. "What's up?"

"I, um, kinda messed up my card. The one from your class. Do you have any more of the kits?"

"No. The class was full enough that I only had a handful left, and I gave those to Graciela to sell at the store."

"Oh." I could hear the disappointment in Nikki's voice. "I already checked with Graciela. She said she sold them all already."

"Really?" Despite everything, my spirits rose a little at that. If my designs were popular enough to sell out in a couple of days, maybe my dream of ditching the corporate world for my true passion wasn't as far off as I feared. Suddenly, I had an itch to talk to Graciela about who had bought the kits, and whether there had been any more demand. "I'll tell you what. I'll head over to the store now and put together a few more kits. Then I'll ask Graciela to put one aside just for you, and you can pick it up when you get off work. You can swing by Central Paper on your way home, right?" Nikki was the bookkeeper for her father's bookstore.

"Sure. Could you ask her to save two for me? Just in case I screw up again?"

I chuckled—the first time I'd been even *tempted* to laugh all day. "Of course. I'm about to take a lunch break. I'll text you when everything's available."

"Oh, *thank* you, Tash. I'm sorry I'm such a bother—"

"You're not. Every crafter takes a misstep now and then. I won't bore you with tales of all my projects that didn't turn out the way I'd planned."

"Yeah, but when *your* projects don't turn out according to plan, you turn them into something even better."

"That's nice of you to say, honey, but—"

"It's the truth! Even Ava said so."

My breath caught and my grip tightened on my phone. *Why is she using past tense for Ava?* But I shook myself as though I were shedding bad thoughts like Portland's inevitable raindrops. Nikki was probably just referring to a statement Ava had made in the past, not that Ava herself was in the past.

Even though she was.

"I've got to run. I'll let you know when you can pick up your card kits."

"Thank you, Tash. Really. For this and the other night and, well, everything."

"Sure, honey. Talk to you soon."

As I tossed my phone in my bag, I spotted Neal and Gil, our CFO, in earnest conversation outside Gil's office. They both glanced my way, so before they could pounce on me and ask me to do something else that was totally outside my job description, I high-tailed it out of my office and took the elevator down to the basement where Vinh lorded over the IT team like the ruler of a subterranean race.

PJ wasn't at his desk, nor were any of Vinh's other tech troglodytes. But Jazz, the DBA, was in their corner cubicle, AirPods visible under their shoulder-length raspberry tipped locs, typing away as they frowned at the three giant monitors on their sit-to-stand desk.

"Hey, friend." I leaned my palm on their desk—it was in stand mode, but Jazz was a tiny thing, only about five feet nothing on a good day, so standing for them would be more like crouching for me.

They pulled out their AirPods with a grin. "Hey, ma. Looking for your boy?" When I nodded, they gestured to the room. "Vinh's got everyone at the co-location, freaking out about the new servers."

"But not you?"

Their big white grin was smug. "It's Software Patch Tuesday. I've got scripts to run. Besides, Vinh knows better than to pull me in on a hardware crisis. Data, yes. Hardware, no."

"Thanks, Jazz. Good luck with Patch Tuesday." Of course, now that made me think of the investigation again because of Huber's quilter wife. Lord, the places my brain could take me.

But my lunch hour was ticking away, so I said goodbye to Jazz and hurried out to my car. I scanned the lot for Moocher, but if PJ was at the co-location, he'd probably have driven. Vinh liked to load the team into his minivan and chauffeur them all like a cranky bus driver, but PJ always resisted. He said it made him feel like he was on a chain gang.

As I drove to Central Paper, I ran through a mental list of required items in addition to the card supplies. With my basic kit impounded, there were a few things I needed. Like most serious crafters, I had a backup kit, but it didn't have some of the latest and greatest things I'd picked up recently. When I parked next to the store, I realized the one advantage of not having PJ along—he couldn't give me grief about buying more supplies that he claimed were unnecessary.

I froze, my hand hovering over the ignition button, remembering something I'd heard at a craft show once. A quilter had laughed and said, "We quilters have a saying—she who dies with the most fabric wins."

Ava had more supplies than any three people. But I couldn't imagine that her last thoughts before she died were *I win*.

CHAPTER FIFTEEN

When I walked into the store, Graciela had just finished ringing up a large sale, if the size of the bag she handed to the customer was any indication. She said goodbye to the customer, then hustled out from behind the counter to give me a hug.

"Hola, *mija*." She kissed my cheek. "Have you come to work your magic again?"

"My magic?"

She grinned. "Take a look around. The last two days have been my busiest for the entire year, and all because of you. Many of the students from your class have come back more than once, and those that you helped last night as well. You are by far my best salesperson and you're not even on my payroll!"

I forced a chuckle. "I just want to help."

"Then you have succeeded." She winked. "If you want to negotiate a commission—"

This time, I laughed more heartily. "Nothing like that. But Nikki called and wanted a couple more of the card kits from the class. She said you'd sold them all?"

"Yes. I sold the first one yesterday morning, and the very next customer bought the other four." Graciela giggled. "I thought she would tackle the woman who bought the other one and snatch the bag out of her hands."

"Yes, some people like to make more than one of the same card. I do it myself, especially if I've got a particular event or occasion."

She waved me off and retreated behind the counter. "I've already had requests for more, so go. Put together many kits, as many as you like."

"I'm on my lunch break so I don't have *that* much time. But I promised Nikki you'd save two of them for her."

"Of course, of course."

Another customer approached with an armful of purchases, so I left Graciela to handle the sale. I had to admit that despite the upsets of the last few days—especially yesterday—I was pleased the store was so busy. I wanted Graciela to be a success, not just for the scrapbooking circle's benefit, but for her own sake as well.

I snagged one of the shopping baskets from inside the front door and cruised over to the paper racks to find the holiday paper I'd used for the cards. I shook my head—I couldn't help it. I loved Graciela to pieces, but she really needed a better inventory display system. I finally found the papers I wanted— textured swirly green for the trees and the glittery gold for the stars—under a stack of blending sponges and rescue dog-themed embellishments. I collected the red ribbon, snowflake die, and a fine-tipped bottle of gloss, and then headed over to the table in the rear of the store where the scrapbooking group always met.

Humming a little "Holly Jolly Christmas," I borrowed one of Graciela's floor-sample Cuttlebugs and used the Christmas tree, star, and snowflake dies to cut all the pieces I needed for each kit. Once all my cutting was done, I sorted the supplies into self-sealing cellophane bags. A woman in jeans and a *Crafting is My Superpower* T-shirt wandered over. "Oooh. What are those?"

"Kits for a Christmas tree and snowflake card." I grinned at her. "With a touch of holiday whimsy."

"Really?" She ran a tentative finger across the textured green paper. "Are they for sale? I've got a dozen people on my list that I want to send specialty cards to."

I hadn't planned on making *that* many kits, and our conversation was attracting attention from other shoppers, but I wasn't about to pass up a chance to boost Graciela's sales. "What about this? I'll show you where the supplies are and we can assemble the kits together." There went my lunch break, but all in a good cause.

"Is this a class?" A woman in a paint-splattered denim shirt and black yoga pants, whom I recognized from the Sunday class, approached the table, her basket clutched to her middle. "I didn't know you offered them during the week."

I laughed. "I don't. This is just a little lunchtime errand." I gestured to the others who had gathered around. "But you're all welcome to join me if you like."

The first woman and the one from the class nodded eagerly. Two more joined us as I took them around the store to gather their supplies, so when we settled back at the table, there were five of us, although several customers lingered to watch as well.

"Okay, Ms. Superpower, you're now the official tree-cutter." I scanned the women sitting at the table as well as the onlookers. "How many kits do we need to make? Everyone hold up their fingers." I counted them up—Ms. Superpower wanted five just on her own—and couldn't help the little glow of satisfaction that people liked my designs. Today, I'd take all the positive reinforcement I could get.

I turned to Ms. Paint-Splatter. "It's Helen, isn't it?"

She beamed at me. "You remember my name? I didn't think you noticed me with all the other, um"—her cheeks pinked—"other fuss."

I returned her smile, although the memory of who caused the *fuss* probably made it look a bit strained. "I make an effort to remember all my students' names. I can't promise to succeed, but I do try." The onlookers surrounding us shifted a little, a couple of them moving closer to observe Ms. Superpower work her Cuttlebug, one or two edging toward the rear. "Helen, if you would please cut one large and two small snowflakes for each kit, we can put them together for everyone who wants one." Helen nodded and got to work with the second Cuttlebug.

Over the soft crunch of dies cutting through the paper and the squeak of the Cuttlebug handle, Ms. Superpower giggled. "This is more fun than I've had in a long time. It's nice to hang out with other crafters. Sometimes I feel so isolated in my home crafting room that I might as well be in Antarctica."

"Yes, this is wonderful," Helen said. "I wish I had a regular crafting support group. I have all these ideas, but sometimes I get stuck and wish I had another set of eyes to give me input on my projects."

I stifled the urge to issue an open invitation to the scrapbooking circle. I'd learned the hard way that new members required vetting. Simple interest or even enthusiasm didn't always mean someone would fit with the rest of the group. Besides, even the current group didn't always get along—Ava and Virginia's perpetual feud being a case in point.

My hand trembled, and I nearly dropped a blob of gloss in the wrong spot. *I guess that feud has ended.* My vision blurred a little, and I blinked away a random tear—because how ridiculous was it that I was about to cry because of a fight that *wouldn't* exist?

Helen put the last snowflake into the last bag. "Wasn't there some kind of bling too? Red gems of some sort?"

"Shoot," I muttered, startling somebody for the second time that day, this time a vaguely familiar woman in a black hoodie who'd stayed to watch from behind the other observers. I recognized her as one of the Brittanys from my class—the non-chatty one who hadn't bothered to start her card. I didn't hold it against her; some people didn't like to work with others watching. I grimaced. For the class cards, I'd used the red embellishments I'd scored at Dianne's booth on Saturday, and the leftovers were all in my basic kit—currently in police custody. "You're absolutely right. Let me show you where Graciela keeps her gems."

Helen's face fell. "Don't you have any of the ones from the class? They were so beautiful. And not like anything here."

"I don't. Not now. But if you're not in a hurry, I think I might be able to get some more." She nodded enthusiastically, and I smiled at her. "Wait here for just a moment then."

I ducked into the back room for a little privacy—I knew Graciela wouldn't mind—to call Dianne. Although she did most of her business at shows and with vendors, she was local, so I crossed my fingers that she'd sell to me directly.

"Hi, Dianne. This is Tash Van Buren. We met at the Expo Center on Saturday? You attended my class on Sunday?"

"Oh, Tash!" Dianne's voice held warmth and welcome, which I counted as a good sign. "You were my good luck charm. I sold more at that show than at any in the past two years, plus I have an appointment with your friend Graciela to talk about stocking a display at her store."

"That's great!" I wandered along a counter stacked with boxes. "I'm calling to beg a favor, actually."

"Anything. You name it."

"Well, I used some of the embellishments I bought at your booth for the class on Sunday, and I've had requests for additional kits. But my remaining supply is, er, unexpectedly unavailable, so I was hoping I could convince you to sell me some more in person."

"Of course. I'm out making vendor calls this afternoon so I've only got samples with me, but I'll be home by four if you'd like to come on by."

"I'm on my lunch break at the moment anyway. Could I drop by after work?" I calculated how early I could escape today. "Around five fifteen or so?"

"Absolutely. If I don't answer the door, it's because I'm out back in the garden, so just come on around. Here's my address."

She rattled it off, but in a store full of paper, I didn't have anything to write on. I pulled a crumpled scrap out of the trash and jotted it down, then read it back to her to make sure I'd got it right. "That's it. See you this evening."

"Thanks, Dianne. You're a peach." As I hung up, I was a little comforted that even though I'd lost one friend, I'd gained another.

I left the back room and rejoined the ladies at the table. Most of the shoppers who'd been watching had already wandered off. "Good news! I should be able to get more of those fabulous gems to bling up your cards. How many do we need?" Everyone counted up their cards, and I added the total to the paper with Dianne's address. "I'll pick them up from the vendor this evening and drop them back here so you can buy them from Graciela. But for now"—I glanced at my watch—"I've got to get back to the Evil Day Job."

The women all chuckled, and Ms. Superpower said, "If you think it's that evil, maybe you should look for another job." She grinned and brandished her basket. "Like helping us all with our crafts."

I wish. But dreams didn't pay the rent. I said goodbye to my impromptu students and walked up to the register. Graciela was between customers, so I laid the mostly completed kits on the counter. "These aren't quite done, but I need some supplies from Dianne."

"Oh, yes. The lady from the show. I'm meeting her for tea this afternoon as soon as Kim arrives for her shift." Graciela chuckled. "She told me that until you started *pulling* for her, her booth was as lively as a graveyard."

Graveyard. I swallowed to ease the tightness in my throat. "No. I think there was just some weird timing thing. The show was empty, and then suddenly this massive wave of people just crashed through the doors." I wrinkled my nose. "Well, not *crashed*, precisely." Other than the two people who seemed determined to knock me or PJ over. "But it was definitely a sudden rush."

She tapped the side of her nose, nodding sagely. "I bet I know what that was. The police, they had the roads blocked over by Lloyd Center. They were even diverting traffic off I-5. It was a mess."

PJ had mentioned something similar as the reason he was late. I dug my debit card out of my purse. "Do you know what caused it?"

"I'd heard that it was—ay, *Dios mio!*" She glared at me and waved my debit card away. "What is this insult? Your money is no good here." She winked. "Not when I can sell these with such a markup, about which not one person will complain."

I shook my head, but I wasn't really annoyed. Markup for a value-add service was completely reasonable—and critical for a business with such slim margins. "If I can't drop the last pieces off after I visit Dianne this evening, I'll stop in tomorrow." I gestured to the women who'd joined me at the table. "Just so you know, I'm getting enough for everyone."

She snorted. "Of course you are."

"Now you sound like PJ," I said with a laugh. PJ, who was probably so deep in server hell that he hadn't stopped for lunch. I had just enough time to pick up Subway sandwiches for both of us—after all, it's not as though eating at my desk was an unusual event.

I moved aside so that Ms. Superpower could step up to the register. I waved at Graciela. "I'll see you later, hon." She blew me a kiss as I pushed through the door in a cheerful tinkle of bells.

CHAPTER SIXTEEN

Back at the office, after I dropped PJ's spicy Italian sandwich off on his desk, I scarfed down my own veggie sub while I scrolled past a dozen emails from Neal, all of which had garbled references to "fun" in the subject line. I ignored them, because fun was the last thing on my mind with a full afternoon of polishing my product launch deliverables ahead of me.

At four thirty, he bopped into my office again. "Well?"

I tore my gaze away from a new spec sheet from design engineering that completely trashed the afternoon's work. "Well what?"

"My suggestions for your Fun Committee. Did you like them? I sent you some emails."

Fun Committee? *My* Fun Committee? *I'll deal with that later.* "I haven't read them."

Neal gaped at me. "But Tash, we've got to get cracking on those morale boosters, those excitement builders. The company picnic. T-shirts. Stress balls. Water bottles." His eyes had taken on a manic gleam. "We have to get this party *started.*"

By *we*, he clearly meant me. "Neal—"

"The Portland Best survey is next month."

Ah ha. So that's *it.* Neal had been dying to get the company on the *Portland Business Journal's* list of top places to work since the day I started here. I sighed. There was no way I could convince him that slapping on *fun* Band-Aids in the name of morale would not fix the company's workability issues.

Those started at the top.

I stood up. "We'll sort this out tomorrow."

"But, Tash—"

"Listen, Neal, the vendor we use for promotional materials like T-shirts and stress balls is in New Jersey. They're closed. We can't do a damn thing about it until tomorrow morning, and in the meantime, I've got an appointment."

I shoved my laptop into my work tote, grabbed my purse, and strode past a still-gaping Neal. Once down the hall and out of his sight, I checked my cell phone. The only message from PJ was a single emoji string—dynamite, knife, bomb, and six exploding heads—so clearly his day had been just as delightful as mine. I stopped by the IT bullpen on my way out, but the place was empty except for Howard, the third shift help desk guy, perched on his balance ball chair.

The bag with PJ's lunch was missing from his desk, and I was relieved that he'd at least had a chance to eat. Then I spotted Howard with his mouth full, bread crumbs caught in his beard, fumbling the bag into his trash can.

"Howard. Are you eating PJ's sandwich?"

Howard's eyes bulged behind his black-framed glasses as he chewed and swallowed. He wiped his hands on his Watchmen T-shirt. "Be fair, Tash. It was just going to waste. It wouldn't have been any good tomorrow."

"Did you at least ask him if you could have it?"

His gaze shifted away. "Well. No. But he could have taken it with him when he blew through here this afternoon."

I frowned. "He was here and didn't take his lunch?"

He shrugged. "Maybe he already ate."

PJ *never* turned down a spicy Italian sub. If he'd passed it up this time, his day must have been even worse than mine. "Next time, Howard"—I pointed at his nose, making his eyes cross—"*ask first.*"

"Right. Sorry, Tash."

I hustled out to my car. If I didn't hit traffic, I'd actually be early for a change. But of course it had to be one of *those* days, and 99W was a solid line of cars from I-5 to 217. While I was stopped at the light by the Tigard Cinemas, I called Dianne to let her know I'd be late, but the call went to voicemail so I left a message.

By the time I got to her place, it was nearly six-thirty. Her house was a two-story home with a bay window and rustic brown shutters, situated at the apex of a cul-de-sac. For a smallish house, it was on a surprisingly large lot, and it was obvious from the trees rising between her yard and her neighbors on either side that it was private. I parked on the street, peering at the windows. It was still broad daylight—June days in Portland didn't end until after nine—so it wasn't surprising that there were no lights on inside.

Despite being a bit late, I couldn't help stopping on my way to the front door to admire Dianne's flowerbeds. A grab-bag of heirloom flowers were blooming in well-tended profusion. I wanted a house someday, and when I got it, I planned to have a garden just like this—as colorful and well laid out as a scrapbook page.

I climbed the porch steps and rang the bell. The chime echoed inside, but I couldn't hear any movement. I waited a minute or so, then rang again for good measure. When there was still no response, I grinned. Dianne must be in her back garden, and sue me, I was dying to see it. If her tiny front yard looked this wonderful, I could imagine what a woman with Dianne's color sense would do with more space.

I followed the path past the flowerbeds to a tall gate set in a weathered cedar fence. It was slightly ajar—nice of Dianne to leave it on the latch for me. When I pushed it open, all my expectations were met and exceeded.

"Wow," I breathed. The decorative brick path was lined with larkspur and bellflowers, bees buzzing busily in their blooms.

The back yard was roughly pie-shaped—although from an extremely generous pie—with the narrower end near the house, its back deck cutting a bite out of the pie slice. Below the deck, the path broadened into a terrace, the bricks arranged in a basket-weave pattern. And the flowers! It was as though I'd been transported to an English country garden. My historical romance writer friends would absolutely *love* this place. I could just imagine sitting on the terrace with a cup of tea and some of my friend Margaret's perfect scones.

But as beautiful as the place was, it was also deserted. "Dianne? It's Tash," I called. I glanced back at the house. A set of French doors opened off the deck, but they were closed and I couldn't detect any movement inside. There was a garden shed at the furthest corner of the lot, fronted by a wisteria-covered pergola. Perhaps Dianne was inside and didn't hear my call. I was familiar with that scenario, since PJ often didn't hear me knock at his door if he had his AirPods in—that's one of the reasons we had keys to each other's apartments.

Next to the fence was a strip of grass that led directly to the shed. But the brick path continued on the other side of the terrace, winding through the garden, so I decided to take the scenic route—because how could I resist?

I strolled along, the drone of the bees a soothing background hum as I catalogued all the plants I recognized and snapped pictures of ones I didn't. A rambling rose trailed over an ornamental boulder, its flowers perfuming the air. Fluffy pink peonies and deep blue delphiniums were backed by spikes of white and yellow hollyhocks. Lavender, of course—what country garden would be complete without it?—and Dianne had a wide swath of it, nestled in a curve of the path, although there was a gap in the cluster of plants. Maybe she'd harvested some of it for potpourri. I couldn't remember any dried flowers at her booth, but I'd been distracted. As I got closer, the scent grew heavier in the warm air, and the buzzing louder. When I leaned down to touch a lavender sprig, a bee shot out at me and I jumped back.

It zipped around me angrily and I realized it wasn't a bee at all—it was a yellow jacket wasp. Yellow jackets were scavengers more than pollinators, and I couldn't imagine Dianne would allow a nest to persist in her lovely garden. Several more shot out of the lavender.

And then I saw what had drawn them.

Face down in the lavender, still wearing garden gloves, a shovel near her outstretched hand and a straw hat half-crushed under her head, was Dianne. And with the number of yellow jackets crawling over her face and arms, she was obviously dead.

I stumbled back a step, my stomach turning over, although I somehow managed not to lose my lunch in the lavender. My phone was still clutched in my hand from all the plant pictures I'd been taking, so I dialed 9-1-1 with shaky fingers.

"9-1-1. What is your emergency?"

"I've just discovered a friend's b-body." Despite the warmth of the afternoon and the sweat prickling the back of my neck, my teeth were chattering. "In her garden."

"Is she breathing?"

I forced myself to look again. *Damn my need to verify results.* "Definitely not." I gave the operator my name and the address and promised to stay on the line until the police arrived, wishing like crazy that PJ were here for moral support. I wanted to shoo the yellow jackets away, but the last thing I needed was to have them go for me—yellow jackets were vindictive little monsters—and besides, I might compromise yet another death scene.

"Oh, lord. Two bodies in two days." It was a good thing PJ *wasn't* here. I could just imagine what he'd say about this: *"Discovering one body is an unlucky chance, LaTashia. Discovering two in as many days is a* pattern.*"*

"I'm sorry, Ms. Van Buren. I didn't catch that," the operator said.

"Nothing." I smacked my forehead. All 9-1-1 calls were recorded and now I was on tape mumbling about not one but two dead bodies.

"The police are on their way."

"Thank you." I retreated up the path to a rustic bench next to a bed of poppies. For a minute or two, I sat there alternately sweating and shivering. I glanced down at my phone. I couldn't call PJ while keeping the 9-1-1 operator on the line, but I could still text him. Because after this, I'd *really* need a drink, not to mention a little quality BFF time. I prided myself on being capable and confident, but two bodies in two days? It might not be a pattern, but it was definitely painful.

I checked my phone—still nothing from PJ other than the earlier emoji explosion, not even a response to my text about picking up lunch for him. Of course, he didn't always respond immediately if he was in full geek mode, hip-deep in some knotty network problem.

I hesitated, my finger poised over the message app. What would I tell him? It's not as though he could do anything about it. And despite my desire to have a hand to hold—and knowing PJ, he'd drop everything to come to my aid, network crisis be damned—if *me* discovering two deaths in two days was an unfortunate coincidence, having *both* of us on the scene twice would stretch even PJ's *Forensic Files*-honed imagination.

"Ms. Van Buren?"

I startled at the deep voice, nearly dropping the phone, and looked up into Detective Bae's dark eyes. I had a brief mental image of PJ sighing over his Detective Hottie again as I struggled to my feet to face him and Detective Huber. I held the phone to my ear to let the dispatcher know the police had arrived and to disconnect the call.

Bae winced a little. Had Huber jabbed him with her elbow? "You discovered the victim?"

I nodded and pointed to the lavender. "She's over there."

The two of them walked far enough down the path to be able to see Dianne's body, then Huber spoke into her cell phone. She must have been giving the crime scene team directions, because a few minutes later, two people in the usual hazmat suits trooped down the path with their equipment bags. This time, they were wearing hoods that looked like mosquito netting. Huber must've warned them about the yellow jackets.

The medical examiner's team wasn't too far behind. I pressed my hand to my chest as two men trundled a gurney down the brick path. That gurney would soon hold a body bag filled with the remains of a beautiful woman taken far, far too soon.

A quaint cottage, lush garden, and thriving crafting business were all on my bucket list of life goals. Dianne was—*had been*—living my dream. She was *me* only now she was gone. Tears rolled down my cheeks. *If only I'd been earlier.* Would it have made a difference? Had Dianne died alone because the 99W traffic had kept me from being on the spot when she needed help?

Bae strode back to me. "Ms. Van Buren, if you could come with me while the teams work? I have some questions." For a second, his features seemed to soften with sympathy before shifting back to their usual chiseled granite.

"Of course." I pulled a lace-trimmed handkerchief from my purse, dabbed my cheeks, then blew my nose like a trumpet. Not very elegant or ladylike, but I was beyond caring about appearances. *PJ would be appalled.*

I followed him up the path and around the side of the house. His car was blocking the end of Dianne's driveway. He gestured to it. "Would you like to sit?"

I wanted to say no, but my knees wobbled. *To hell with staying strong.* "Yes, please."

CHAPTER SEVENTEEN

Bae opened the back door, and I sat sideways, smoothing my skirt over my knees. I crossed my ankles and focused on my shoes. *Pink. Pointed toes. Kitten heels. They always make me feel better, so why aren't they working now?*

Stupid question. I knew why. My throat worked as I fought back tears.

He hunkered down in front of me. "Who is the victim?"

"Her name is Dianne Detwiler."

"How do you know her?"

"I don't. Well, not well. I only met her on Saturday when I was at the craft show with A-Ava." My voice broke, and I had to blink rapidly for a bit. "She was a vendor."

"Was Mr. Purdy with you?"

I frowned, trying to remember whether PJ had joined us by then. "Not the first time Dianne and I spoke. But maybe later? Why?"

He shifted uneasily—it couldn't have been comfortable crouching down like that. "Just routine questions. So you purchased items from her at the show?"

"Yes. Ava and I both did. Dianne had a lovely selection of... of..." Oh, lord. Dianne was *dead*. A sob caught me unprepared, and it was all over.

I'm not opposed to crying in general, and PJ could vouch that I'm no stranger to causing a scene, since he's usually part of it—

only he christens them *events*. But typically our *events* were well orchestrated with impeccable costuming.

This was nothing like that.

This wasn't an event. This was most definitely a *scene*—a full-out, one hundred percent, mountain-of-tissues *ugly* cry. A loud, tear-stained, snot-filled ugly cry. I covered my face with my hands and hunched forward, my tears slipping between my fingers to plop onto my skirt. I heard the rustle of Bae's suit and the *snick* of the car door opening.

"Here." His normally brusque voice was gentler. I lowered my hands to see him holding out a little packet of tissues.

Much more practical than a lace-edged hanky. At this point, all hope of maintaining my upbeat retro-glam persona was long gone, and more than anything? I needed to blow my nose. So I accepted them—they were the extra large, extra soft kind. "Thank you," I croaked. "Are these department issue?"

His poker face actually cracked a little, amusement and maybe exasperation flickering over it. "No."

I blotted the tears off my cheeks. "Thank Detective Huber for me."

"They, ah, weren't her idea." He didn't meet my gaze—and were his cheeks a little pinker? My, my. Detective Hottie had a marshmallow center under his crunchy outer shell. I made a mental note to tell PJ.

I honked into the tissue—okay, I honked into several of them. But as much as I'd rather find a nest of pillows to crawl into and pretend none of this was happening, it was time to get back to adulting. I stuffed the tissues into the handy trash receptacle in Bae's car, took a deep breath and stood up.

"Thank you." I managed a not-too-watery smile. "If you keep these on hand as a way of reassuring witnesses, it's working."

He cleared his throat. "Yes. Well. Can you tell me about discovering Ms. Detwiler this evening? Why were you here?"

"I used the embellishments I purchased from Dianne in a class I taught on Sunday."

"That would be the same class where you saw Ms. Cornell for the last time?"

"Yes. The Christmas card class." I had to swallow again, and tugged another tissue out of the packet, just in case. "One of my students contacted me earlier today because her card hadn't turned out the way she wanted and she needed another kit. I went to Central Paper on my lunch break to put one together for her."

"Was Mr. Purdy with you at that time? You work together, I believe."

I squinted at him. "Yes, but we're not joined at the hip. I'm in product marketing. PJ is a systems engineer. He works in internal IT. Besides, he's not a fan of paper crafts."

"Yet he was with you at the Expo Center and at your class, correct?"

That damn goose was back, doing a salsa dance on my grave. "He's my best friend. He was *supporting* me."

His poker face was back. "Of course. Please go on."

"While I was putting together the kits—"

"I thought you were only making the one your student needed."

"Graciela asked me to put together a few more for her to sell. She's sold all the extras I left with her on Sunday."

"I see."

"While I was assembling them, a number of customers came over and joined me. I helped them find the materials in the store, but then realized that I didn't have the embellishments I needed." I lifted an eyebrow. "They're in my bag, which you impounded yesterday." He made a noncommittal sound. "I had Dianne's business card, and I knew she was local, so I called and asked if I could buy some more directly from her. We arranged for me to stop by this evening."

"Why did you go into the garden?"

I narrowed my eyes again. "Am I a suspect, Detective?"

He may have sighed. "You were the first person on the scene. I'm simply trying to determine the sequence of events."

"When I called at lunchtime, Dianne invited me to come over right away but I had to return to work so we arranged to meet later. She told me to come around to the garden if she didn't answer the door. She didn't."

"Did you discover her immediately?"

I bit my lip, my stomach protesting a little over my memory of how I'd strolled around, enjoying the garden, while Dianne had been lying there at the mercy of the yellow jackets. "No. I called out, but she didn't answer, so I was making my way toward the shed at the far corner of the yard. I thought she might be in there." I swallowed. "I called 9-1-1 as soon as I found her."

Bae remained poker-faced as usual. "What time did you last speak to her?"

"Probably between twelve forty-five and one o'clock. Oh!" I dug in my purse and pulled out the receipt for the Subway sandwiches. "I bought lunch right after I left the store and I'd spoken to Dianne less than ten minutes before that."

He took it but didn't look at it. "Wouldn't the exact call time be logged on your phone?"

My cheeks heated. *Of course it would.* I checked my phone. "Twelve fifty-three. Sorry. I'm a little rattled."

"No need to apologize. Do you have any idea what else Ms. Detwiler might have planned before your appointment?"

Actually, I did. But if I told Bae about Graciela's meeting with Dianne, would that put her under suspicion? If I didn't say anything, though, it would obstruct the investigation, and I wanted whoever did this to Dianne caught before someone else got hurt. "The owner of Central Paper told me she had a meeting with Dianne this afternoon to discuss placing some of Dianne's products in the store. I don't know if the meeting took place. But I'm sure she'd never hurt anyone."

"Mmmphmm." Really, Bae should patent that noise because it gave *nothing* away. He peered at the receipt. "Interesting that you assume foul play."

I propped my hands on my hips. "You're the one who told us that any death scene is treated as a potential homicide until the coroner declares otherwise."

He didn't respond to the tartness of my tone, but he peered down at the receipt. "Two sandwiches?"

"I bought one for PJ since he couldn't get away." I remembered Howard scarfing down PJ's favorite spicy Italian sub. "Not that he had a chance to eat it."

"You gave it to him personally?"

"No. I left it on his desk. One of his coworkers ate it when PJ didn't—" My eyes widened. "Wait a minute. You can't possibly think that PJ had anything to do with this!" I pointed at Bae's chest. "In the first place, he's not the kind of person to do anything remotely violent. In the second place, he barely knew Dianne. In the third, he was tied up with a server crisis all day, which I'm sure his boss or the other people on his team could verify."

Bae pretended to ignore my finger, but his expression was definitely more testy and affronted than inscrutable. "We're simply gathering as much information as we can about these cases." He flinched—only slightly, and he recovered quickly, but PJ claimed I could read a person's body language like a graphic novel.

"You think this is connected to Ava's murder, don't you?"

His stone face was back. "I can't comment on any ongoing investigation."

"You do. Oh my god. That's... that's..." I threw up my hands. "I don't even know what to say."

"Mmmphmm."

I huffed an exasperated breath. "Fine. Can you at least tell me if Ava's passing is public knowledge yet?"

He nodded. "We've notified her daughter. She'll be here tonight or tomorrow. And the news of Ms. Cornell's death has been released."

"Good." It was my turn to cringe. "Well, not *good* in the sense of the news itself, but I'd like to express my condolences to Rebecca, and I know the rest of our scrapbooking circle would as well."

"You may discuss the fact of her death, but please don't disclose any information about its nature."

"I'm not an idiot, Detective." My words as well as my tone probably weren't the most sensible, but the ME team had just rounded the corner of the house with the body bag. Another sob was fighting to get out, and I *refused* to break down again—being assertive was one of my go-to techniques for getting through emotional scenes with authority figures without showing weakness.

"No. You're very astute." He spread his palms. "But it's our standard warning, and I'd be remiss if I didn't deliver it." One of the white-suited crime scene techs came over to Bae and handed him a plastic evidence bag.

It held two tiny teal feathers.

Bae's expression turned briefly furious before he schooled it into its default calm. He glanced over at Huber, who was standing by the gate, and nodded. She turned away, lifting her phone to her ear.

Now there's a thing you should know about me—my Auntie Willa Mae always claimed to have the Sight, and while I wouldn't go that far, I can't deny that sometimes I get *feelings*.

And I was getting a very bad feeling right now. I started shaking so badly that I almost didn't feel my phone vibrating. The screen didn't display a number I knew, but my *feeling* warned me that it wasn't a call about lowering my credit card interest rate or a timeshare scam.

"Hello?"

"Hey, Tash." PJ's voice was shaking as much as I was. "I've been arrested. Could you do me a favor and feed my cat?"

CHAPTER EIGHTEEN

PJ was always teasing me about my vast array of connections. If it wasn't the Kevin Bacon thing, he was likening me to an infinite network hub. He'd tried the spider/spiderweb analogy once, but I'd shut that one down hard. Because spiders. No. Just no.

But Kevin Bacon, network hubs, or spiderwebs, I was never so grateful to have resources at my fingertips.

My first call was to my lawyer friend Forrest, who owed me big time. I helped him make a scrapbook that he used to propose to his wife—more than five hundred photographs, chronicling their relationship from high school through law school. So yeah. Big time. And if it meant lassoing one of the best criminal defense lawyers in town for PJ's benefit, I wasn't above calling in that favor.

Next, a friend of a friend was besties with the wife of the Washington County jail warden. So before the sun set on one of the longest days ever, Forrest and I were seated an interrogation room.

Given my last-minute summons, Forrest was surprisingly well put together in his gray bespoke suit and Captain America tie, his ginger goatee perfectly trimmed. But then, maybe dressing for intimidation was his lawyer superpower. He was as calm as I was jittery, his fountain pen held motionless over his legal pad while my heels clicked against the concrete floor as my knees bounced.

When the guard escorted PJ into the room, I almost didn't recognize him. For one thing, he was wearing an orange jumpsuit, and as PJ has told me more times than I can count, jumpsuits are only good on *Star Trek* and orange is *not* his color. For another, he... drooped. His shoulders, his hair, the corners of his mouth—all his usual verve was damped down so far it was undetectable.

Plus, he was handcuffed.

He'd never looked so much like he needed a hug—and of course, because of the jail rules, I couldn't give him one.

The guard led him to the table by one elbow. "Half an hour," the guard said, and then stepped outside. A glass window allowed him to keep an eye on us, but the door allowed enough isolation to meet attorney-client privilege regulations.

I clutched my pearls so I wouldn't violate rules and reach across the table to grab his hand. "Oh, honey. I'm so sorry. But don't worry. With Forrest's help, we'll get this straightened out in no time."

PJ's smile was wan. "Will we?"

"Of course! You didn't hurt Dianne. I don't know what Bae is thinking."

"Not just Dianne." He pushed his lank hair off his forehead with both hands, causing his handcuffs to clink. "Ava too."

"What?" I screeched. Unfortunately, that caught the attention of the guard, but I waved at him. "All good." Then I leaned forward and whispered, "How can they possibly think that?"

For an instant, the light returned to PJ's eyes in a militant sparkle. "It's that stupid boa's fault. They found feathers."

"Hold on, you two," Forrest interjected. "Tash filled me in on everything that has transpired up to this point, but let's hit pause for a moment. What's the significance of finding feathers and how does that make you a suspect?"

I sighed. "We attended the big craft show at the Expo Center last weekend. PJ got a teal feather boa from one of the vendors." I jabbed the table with my index finger. "Of course they found feathers at Ava's. You were wearing the boa, and it was shedding like a molting hen."

PJ grimaced. "They were *under* Ava's body."

Forrest and I blinked at him. "Under? But…" I shook my head. "Whatever. Those feathers went *everywhere*. Bae had one stuck to his eyebrow for at least twenty minutes. They probably blew under there when the CSI team processed the scene."

"Maybe." His shoulders slumped even more. "But that wouldn't account for the ones they found under Dianne."

"Peej—"

"Okay," Forrest interjected again. "Feathers allegedly from your boa were found at both crime scenes under both victims?" When PJ nodded, Forrest uncapped his fountain pen and made notes in something that must be lawyer code because I certainly couldn't make it out.

"You know—" PJ dredged up a ghost of his usual smirk from somewhere. "Spending quality time in handcuffs with Detective Hottie isn't nearly as fun as I expected."

I gritted my teeth, stomach roiling. This was so unfair. "If feathers are the only evidence—"

"Fingerprints. My fingerprints were all over Ava's house."

"Of course they were. We were there for at least ten minutes before we found her."

"But yours weren't."

"I was wearing gloves!"

PJ sighed. "There's traffic cam footage of me in Moocher near the intersection of 99W and Bull Mountain around the time that Dianne…" He glanced at Forrest. "Left this plane of existence."

Forrest paused, his pen suspended over his pad. "And why were you at the intersection of 99W and Bull Mountain?"

"PJ is in the IT department for our company. The co-location data center that houses our servers is less than a mile away. PJ had a perfectly legitimate reason for being there." I snapped my fingers as the obvious solution dawned on me. "That's it! You were working over there with the whole team, right? They can give you an alibi."

"I was there alone most of the afternoon. Vinh"—he nodded at Forrest—"my boss ordered us all back to the server room at the office right after lunch, but sent me back alone afterward. So apparently I had ample opportunity to zip over there, bash Dianne with a shovel, and jab a snowflake into her neck."

"A what?"

He lifted his hands as though he was about to sketch something in the air, but the cuffs clinked and he lowered them again. "A snowflake. You know. One of those dangerous pointy metal things that fits into one of your infernal craft machines."

"You mean a die? Like for the Cuttlebug?"

He clenched his eyes shut. "Please don't use that word."

"Cuttlebug?"

"No." He clenched his teeth. "*Die.*"

I leaned forward, but the table's edge digging into my middle reminded me I couldn't hug him. *Damn it!* "PJ—"

"The snowflake didn't kill her. Not like it killed Ava. But—"

"So Ava was killed by a..." Forrest glanced at his notes. "...a *die* too?"

PJ glared at him. "Ohmygod, I *told* you—"

"PJ, this more than anything proves you couldn't have anything to do with it. You *hate* paper crafts."

PJ snorted. "Apparently that makes it more likely that I'd take out my homicidal tendencies with them, thus proving my hatred for the weapon and the victim simultaneously."

"Mr. Purdy." Forrest capped his pen and set it on the table. "As your attorney, I advise you to *never* repeat that sentiment."

I rubbed my hands over my face. "I really wish you didn't watch so many of those crime shows."

"Believe me," PJ said, his voice shaky, "right now, I wish the same thing."

The guard opened the door and stepped inside. "Time's up." He walked over to cup PJ's elbow and pull him to his feet.

I pushed myself out of the awful plastic chair. "I promise we'll get to the bottom of this."

PJ pressed his lips together as if he was keeping an incriminating comment from bursting out. Then he sighed. "Just promise me you'll take care of Mary Pickford."

"Mary Pickford?"

"My cat, Tash. Just take care of my cat." He smiled tightly and let the guard lead him out.

"This is the most unbelievable, ridiculous, *outrageous*..." I muttered as a deputy escorted Forrest and me from the room. I turned to the deputy. "Where would we find the homicide detectives?"

She glanced from Forrest to me. "You'd have to ask for them at the front desk."

"Well, then, take us there." I offered zero apology for my curtness as she showed us the way. Apparently when my loved ones get arrested, I get a tad testy.

When I demanded to speak to Detective Bae, the staffer behind the desk didn't show me to his lair. Instead, he made a call and Huber showed up.

"Ms. Van Buren. What can I do for you?"

"You can release PJ."

She sighed. "I can't do that. Right now, the evidence supports his arrest, and unless we discover something that tells a different story—"

"Then I'll find it." I straightened my shoulders. "Because I'm telling you, you've got the wrong person."

"Ms. Van Buren. *Tash*." Huber's tone held sympathy edged with warning. "Please do not interfere with the investigation. You could harm Mr. Purdy's case more than you help it."

"Don't worry. I'm not *stupid*. But I know PJ better than anyone, and I know he didn't do this. The police ask for information from the public to assist them, right? Well, I'll do everything in my power to *assist*."

"Tash—"

"Excuse me, but I have a cat to feed." I paused with my hand on the door handle. "And tell Detective Bae for me that he should be ashamed of himself."

She huffed a laugh. "Oh trust me. He is."

Forrest flanked me as I headed for the storage lockers where jail visitors had to check their belongings. *Jail visitors.* I almost cried.

I collected my purse and Forrest his satchel. When we stepped outside into the cool night air, he gave me a reassuring hug. "I've got this covered, Tash."

I leaned into the embrace for a minute, then stepped back. "You don't know how good that makes me feel."

He rubbed the back of his neck. "I have to admit that the details of this case are... interesting, to say the least. I'll review the evidence and have another conversation with Mr. Purdy. We'll get through this. I promise."

He accompanied me to my car, making sure I was inside before he lifted a hand in farewell. I gripped my steering wheel as he walked away. Despite Huber's assurance, I debated whether to call Bae and tell him exactly why he'd made a huge mistake. After all, I still had both his and Huber's cards in my purse, and I was alternating between furious and terrified at PJ's predicament. I really didn't want to think about him locked up in there, with who knows what kind of other people. PJ might talk a confident game, but when it came down to it? He was still... medium. And jail wasn't the safest place for guys who relied on bravado rather than bulk for self-defense.

Only the notion that antagonizing Bae might make things even worse for PJ kept me from making the call. Instead, I drove over to PJ's place. Moocher was parked in his spot under the carport. *Oh, lord. They arrested him at his home.* That meant his neighbors witnessed it. My eyes prickled, and I blinked rapidly.

Poor PJ. He was probably mortified. On the other hand, he probably wouldn't have been crazy about being arrested at work either.

Work. Did Vinh know? I should have asked PJ when I had the chance. I parked my car and sent a quick text to Francine, our HR director. I'd have a quiet word with her tomorrow and find out what the options were. PJ was bound to be released because only an idiot—*Bae*—would believe he could murder anyone, but who knew how long the investigation would take?

I took the stairs up to PJ's door. I gave thanks that he and I were the sort of besties who swapped home and car keys, so at least I didn't have to convince the property manager to let me in. I opened the door carefully. The last thing I needed was to have to chase the cat—*Mary Pickford, PJ? Seriously?*—across the complex.

Of course, the minute I walked in, my nose started to twitch with the urge to sneeze. I really needed to contact the cat rescue people. I followed a trail of teal feathers from the entry to the living room. The boa was coiled on the sofa, and the cat blinked at me from the feathery nest. She kept her gaze fixed on me over the breakfast bar when I stepped into the kitchen. Cans of cat food were lined up in regimental precision on the countertop, and as soon as I popped the lid on one, she leaped off the sofa, raising a veritable hurricane of teal floof.

I sneezed. Between the cat and the feathers, I'd need a respirator by the time I was done here. As Mary Pickford sashayed into the kitchen and wound around my ankles, the feathers clung to my skirt, my shoes, and—I looked cross-eyed —my nose. I blew that one off, only to have it drift into my cleavage.

"I'm surprised the dang boa has any feathers *left*," I muttered as I dug a spoon out of the silverware drawer. "Anyone within ten feet of the thing gets feather-bombed by it faster than they can say 'plucked chicken.'"

I froze with a spoonful of kitty pâté suspended over the cat's dish. *Anyone within ten feet...*

Mary Pickford *mrow*ed irritably and batted at the spoon. I shook the cat food off the spoon into the dish, although part of it landed on her ear. Since I knew for a fact PJ hadn't killed anybody, whoever *had* done the deed had to be someone who'd been near him while he'd been wearing the boa—or at least somewhere he'd been. All the detectives needed to do was trace PJ's movements and interview everyone who'd been in the same place.

I winced as I scooped half the can into the dish, although it wasn't easy with the cat's head in the way. Finding all those people might be a Herculean task. The first place PJ had worn the boa was at the Expo Center, and there were tons of people there—including Dianne and Ava, who both could've been infested with feathers before they ever left the craft show.

I dumped some kibble into the second dish and made sure the water bowl was full. As I washed the spoon, my fingers trembled so much that I dropped it with a clatter, making Mary Pickford leap away from her food for approximately two seconds.

A few of the people on the list were unfortunately too easy for me to identify: Graciela and the women in the scrapbooking circle. Furthermore, Graciela had been scheduled to meet with Dianne the day of the murder. I hated—*hated*—to think that anybody I knew could be capable of not one, but two murders, not to mention framing PJ for the crimes. But it was more important to see that the right person was punished.

And PJ was definitely not the right person.

CHAPTER NINETEEN

When I pulled into the Central Paper parking lot after leaving PJ's apartment, my fingers were clutching the steering wheel so tightly that I practically had to pry them off. It was "Girls' Night In" this evening. Although we couldn't indulge in wine while the store was open, we'd break out our craft du jour, indulge in some high-end chocolate on the side—which Evy usually managed to smear on her project—and *voilà*. Instant party. But instant party was the last thing I wanted tonight. In fact, I'd much prefer to skip the whole thing. As it was, I'd barely have time to greet everyone before the store closed.

Two things got me out of the car and through the front door though. First, the idea of PJ spending one more unnecessary minute in jail if I didn't pursue my own inquiries; and second, that nobody in the group even knew Ava was dead yet.

Except the murderer.

I swallowed against a lump in my throat as the bell chimed with my entrance. The store was busy for this near closing time, and I could hear Evy's chatter from the tables in the back. Graciela grinned at me from behind the register as she was ringing up a sale. "Hola, *mija*. The ladies had almost given you up."

I smiled back, although from the way Graciela's brows drew together, it probably wasn't very convincing. *Could she have done it?* "Sorry. I was a little busy after work."

Her forehead smoothed. "Ah. The evil day job. Go on back. I don't think the ladies have gotten much done tonight." She winked. "Too much to gossip about."

"Gossip?" I croaked. Could it be about the murder? Had the news already broken? "About what?"

But the customer at the register asked Graciela a question. When she turned to answer, I made my way to the crafting tables. Virginia's workspace was as regimented as usual, just as Evy's was its usual chaos, however neither one of them appeared to be actively working on anything.

Nikki just hunched in her chair, toying with a turkey-shaped die. PJ had said the murder weapon was a die. Could Nikki have— *No.* I couldn't see Nikki indulging in any kind of violence. She even winced when she had to cut cardstock using the store's heavy duty paper cutter that we fondly called *La Guillotine.*

"But even though MAX was shut down *forever*, the police couldn't find— Oh, hi, Tash!" Evy grinned up at me brightly. "We were afraid you couldn't make it tonight. We're down two, since Ava didn't make it either."

I checked behind me to make sure none of the other customers were nearby. "I'm afraid I've got some bad news." I swallowed, placing my hand on Evy's shoulder, although I wasn't sure if it was for her comfort or my own. "Ava won't be joining us anymore. She—"

"Don't tell me." Virginia rolled her eyes. "She's bought out all the Graphic 45 *A Proper Gentlemen* paper packs that I was going to use to scrap my father's family tree, refuses to face us, and has convinced you to do the dirty work for her again. Honestly, I could murder that woman."

"Actually…" I took a deep breath. "Ava's dead. She… she was killed on Monday."

"I didn't do it!" Virginia clutched a box of pictures to her chest.

The die in Nikki's hand dropped to the table with a dull clatter. She clapped one hand over her mouth and leaped out of her chair, sending it over backwards, and then raced for the back room, her giant shoulder bag bouncing on her back.

Virginia glanced wildly from Evy, who'd started to cry, to me, to the customers who'd begun craning their necks to see what the commotion was about. She set her pictures down and picked up a pair of Fiskars. "I know I *said* that I wanted to... you know. But that's just something you *say*, not something you *do*."

"We realize that, Virginia." I patted Evy on the back as her sobs grew noisier.

"We've all said something similar more than once." Virginia pointed the scissors at me, and I barely managed to control my wince. "Even your little friend PJ probably did, the way Ava ordered him around."

I gritted my teeth. "That's enough. Nobody is accusing you or me or anyone here. And any *fool*"—*Detective Bae*—"would know PJ couldn't do anything of the kind." I just needed to find some way to convince Bae of said foolishness.

Virginia settled back in her chair, and I breathed a little easier when she put the scissors down. "Good." Her gaze dropped to her work table, and she nudged a Copic pen so it was exactly parallel with the edge of her scrapbook page. "Do you know who's getting her supplies?"

I stepped away from Evy, afraid that my back-patting would get a little too forceful—and it wasn't Evy I was angry with. Virginia's obsession with Ava's crafting stash was bordering on toxic—but could supply envy really prompt somebody to kill?

Virginia certainly had the determination to do anything she put her mind to. But when I remembered the chaos of the crime scene, I checked her off my private list of suspects immediately —she'd never have destroyed so much of what she coveted, let alone have left the room in such a mess. Besides, she hadn't known Dianne, and from what PJ had said, the police were convinced both murders had been committed by the same perpetrator.

"I can't believe it," Evy wailed. Her reaction was definitely starting to attract the attention of other customers, who edged even closer, expressions avid. "We saw her on Sunday and she was perfectly healthy."

"She was *murdered*, you ninny." Virginia slid a jar of bronze embellishments into her kit bag. "She didn't waste away from some mysterious ailment."

Evy ignored Virginia's snide tone, just as she always did. "I know Ava could be, well, *difficult*, but she was generous too. She shared her supplies with me all the time."

"She could afford to," Virginia muttered, "since she bought everything in sight."

"Look." Evy rifled through the scrapbook on the table in front of her, stopping at a mustard yellow page crisscrossed with burnt orange and charcoal gray. "Ava gave me this paper and the shiny gold washi tape for the accents." She leafed to another page, this one navy blue, chocolate brown, and eye-watering neon green. "She made this one for herself but decided it wasn't right for her project so she just gave me the whole thing."

I remembered when Ava made that page. It was on the Naval Academy paper that she'd snagged from under Virginia's nose —and then decided she didn't like after all. I glanced at Virginia, hoping she hadn't seen what Ava had done with it. *Nope. She saw it.*

"Then there's this." Evy pulled the card from my class out of her bag. The corners were crumpled because she'd stuffed it in her craft tote without protecting it, and it sagged in the middle from the weight of the gigantic red embellishment that she'd placed slightly off-kilter. Evy tapped the gem. "On Sunday, she gave me this from her own supplies when she said the ones in the kit weren't—" Evy shot a shamefaced glance at me. "I mean…" She thrust the card at me. "You take it, Tash. I couldn't bear to look at it."

I took it—I couldn't very well refuse—but when Evy's sniffles started to reach epic proportions, I hastily set it on Graciela's discount table so I could hand Evy a tissue. Out of the corner of my eye, I saw one of the hovering customers sidle over to look at the card, then rear back in apparent horror.

I didn't blame them—Evy's projects tended to have that effect on everyone, although it didn't stop people from looking. It was kind of like rubbernecking at a car crash—you were half-afraid to catch sight of something disastrous, but you couldn't look away. In fact, as I stood there, silently handing Evy tissue after tissue—thank goodness Bae had let me keep his stash—a customer with a red hoodie pulled low over her face, her empty basket slung over one arm, peered at it closely, then turned away. From what I could see of her face, her lips were pressed together in apparent disgust.

My throat burned and my eyes prickled for an instant, remembering PJ's tart comments about customers in seasonally inappropriate clothing. PJ could flay someone with a snarky remark, but he'd never, *ever* hurt anybody, let alone kill them.

I vowed to convince Bae and Huber they had the wrong person as a third customer, a young mother with her toddler in a stroller, stopped by the table. But when the child reached for the card—attracted by the shiny object, no doubt—the mom covered the kid's eyes with her hand and wheeled away as if the sight might scar them for life.

In a momentary lull between customers, Graciela hustled over from the register. "What's wrong?" she murmured. "Has something happened to Evy?"

"No." I set Bae's tissues on the table by Evy's elbow and gestured for Graciela to follow me behind a nearby calendar and journal display. I straightened my shoulders as I faced her. She had just as much opportunity to kill Dianne and Ava as PJ did, but I couldn't imagine her doing it any more than him. "It's Ava. She was killed on Monday."

Graciela's hand flew to her mouth. "Ah. *Pobrecita.* Was it a car accident? She was not the most careful of drivers."

"No. She was murdered."

Her eyes rounded. "*Madre de Dios.* Who would do such a thing? People today... *pah!* They think of nobody's pain but their own."

I couldn't remember whether Bae had told me that Dianne's death was public yet. Could I casually ask Graciela if they'd met as planned? But she might ask why I wanted to know—it wasn't exactly a smooth change of subject. Better to leave it until I knew for sure I wouldn't be interfering with the investigation. Besides, one murder at a time was enough for anyone to deal with.

Speaking of which... Nikki still hadn't emerged from the back room. "Excuse me, please. I need to check on Nikki." My height enabled me to peer over the top of the slat wall fixture when the more petite Graciela couldn't. I nodded in the direction of the register. "You've got a line of customers waiting. They'd probably be disgruntled if they all weren't craning their necks to look at Evy."

She waved my words away. "The world will not end if they can't buy their paper and glue in the next two minutes." She hugged me, and my eyes prickled because since PJ's arrest, what I'd missed most was a genuine hug from my best friend. But I returned Graciela's hug anyway, sniffling—although not as intensely as Evy.

Graciela rubbed a soothing circle on my back. "Ava was your friend. I'm sorry that you must be the one to be strong for everyone else. If you need anything—a shoulder, an ear, a strong drink—you may call on me any time."

"Thank you, hon." I released her, a little reluctantly. "I'd better go see about Nikki. The news hit her hard."

"Of course. Of course." She pointed a scarlet-tipped nail at me. "But remember what I said. Anything, anytime." She hurried away.

I straightened my blouse, shook out my skirt, and took a circuitous route through the store so I could avoid the crafting table where—if the sound of Evy's voice was any indication—she was regaling anyone who would listen with tales of Ava's generosity.

CHAPTER TWENTY

Although Graciela's back room was even more cluttered than the relatively spacious store, I was just as familiar with its layout, so I was able to duck through the door and dodge out of sight. I scanned the place, frowning. Some people—Evy most definitely *not* among them—hated for people to see them cry. As shy as Nikki was, she might be one of that number. So where was she?

I headed for the stairs, but as I passed a row of shelves, I caught movement out of the corner of my eye.

Nikki was crouched in front of an open drawer, her back to me and her bag on the floor by her feet. *Oh, lord.* Had she taken advantage of the reaction to Ava's death to steal something else? Could her nervous timidity be all an act? She'd seemed genuinely affected by the news, but I imagined that successful killers would have to be good actors, wouldn't they?

I rubbed my damp palms on my skirt. *These poor donuts are really getting a beating today.* Yesterday—God, had it been only yesterday?—before PJ and I discovered Ava's body, Nikki had talked about doing something "really bad." There wasn't much worse than murder.

Get a grip, Tash. I was starting to see killers under every stack of holiday paper or lurking behind random ink displays. I might have an active imagination—although not as active as PJ's—but I couldn't picture Nikki cutting Ava's throat with a die or bashing poor Dianne with a shovel. Besides, she had no reason to hurt either one of them.

I rose on my toes and crept forward so my heels wouldn't click on the linoleum. "Nikki?"

She startled, and when she whipped her head around to stare at me, she overbalanced and fell onto her butt. A sheaf of pink glitter paper fell out of her hand and fanned across the tiles. "T-Tash?" She pushed herself to her feet. "This isn't what it looks like. I swear."

I moved closer and purposely kept my voice soft. "What do you think it looks like?"

Her hands flopped helplessly at her sides. "You know."

"I've learned that making assumptions about peoples' actions and intent never reflects well—either on me or on them. So why don't you tell me?" Even though I maintained what PJ called my "Mother Tashia" calm demeanor, I admit that I checked the nearby shelves for any sharp objects. Or blunt instruments, for that matter.

Nikki hung her head, scuffing the floor with her grubby white tennis shoes. "It looks like I'm stealing. That's what you thought the other night, isn't it? That I was taking things from Graciela? Things that didn't belong to me?"

"Well…" I hedged.

She sighed. "If you did, you'd have been right. But this time, I'm putting things *back*." She lifted her chin and met my gaze, her eyes wide and desperate. "I wouldn't ever lie to you, Tash. Not you. You've always been so kind. Not judgmental." She slid a glance at the door. "Not like *some* people," she muttered.

"But Nikki, honey, you shouldn't do or not do things for *me*. You should do them for *you*."

Her expression turned earnest. "But that's the thing. I *can* do them for somebody else, somebody who's a good person. I want to be a good person too. But sometimes…" She swallowed and stared at the floor again. "Sometimes there doesn't seem to be any reason to be good. Not when so many other people are bad."

"Does… does doing *bad* things"—and I wasn't sure I wanted to know what bad things Nikki had done, but in for a penny— "make you feel good? Do you *like* doing them? Is that why you do them again?"

Her chin shot up. "No! That's the problem. I don't *like* doing them. I don't even mean to. But sometimes I can't help myself." She gestured to the shelves packed with Graciela's overstock. "I mean, the stuff is just *there* and then before I know it, it's in my bag." Her shoulders slumped, and her mousy hair hung down on either side of her face in lank clumps. "Most of the time, it's not even something I *like*, let alone something I want."

I moved closer and patted her shoulder. "Honey, I'm an engineer, not a psychologist, but don't you think it might be a good idea to get some professional help? I don't mind you using me as an incentive, but I might not always be here."

Panic skittered across her face, and tears welled in her eyes. "Why? Where are you going? Are you moving away? Oh my god, are you *dying*?"

I couldn't help chuckling. "Nothing so dire. I just meant I might not always be *here*." I pointed to the ground. "Nearby. So I think it's probably important for you to work through this with somebody who knows how to address the real issues." I fumbled in my purse for the tissue packet, but remembered I'd left it with Evy. "If your medical insurance doesn't cover counseling, I can help a little."

She sighed. "It does. But if I go through with it, if I talk to a therapist, I'll have to *tell* them. Admit what I've done. What if they look at me like… like *Virginia* would?"

Virginia as a therapist. Now *there* was a scary thought. "It's their job to help you, honey. Not judge you. And if you have the bad luck to land on one who doesn't treat you with respect? Get another one."

She gave a watery chuckle. "It would be just my luck to get one like that."

"I've got several friends who are therapists. If you like, I can ask one of them for a recommendation."

She bit her lip. "Would it have to be somebody you know?"

"Of course not. Not if that would make you uncomfortable."

"It's just... When I tell them, I'm afraid they'll think I'm as bad as those jewel thieves. And I wouldn't want you to think any worse of me than you already do."

I gave her a hug. "First, no reputable counselor would divulge client details to *anybody*, including a friend. Second, I don't think badly of you. Far from it." I patted her back, then moved away. "Third, what jewel thieves?"

She blinked at me. "The ones who— Oh, you weren't there when we were talking about it. You remember that traffic jam on Saturday?"

"And the MAX holdup?" I knelt and started gathering the scattered paper. "Yes. It's why PJ was late meeting me at the Expo Center."

Nikki crouched down beside me, scrabbling glittery sheets into a messy pile. "Uh-huh. Well, there was a rock and gem show at the Convention Center that day, and somebody stole some stuff from one of the exhibits." She handed me her less-than-pristine stack. *Graciela's gonna have to put those on the discount table.* "Rubies. Pretty valuable ones, I guess, because there was a big fuss before they caught—"

"Rubies?" One of the sheets fluttered out of my numb fingers.

Nikki nodded. "Kinda big ones. It was all over the news the other night."

"I haven't really been keeping up." *Oh, my god.* My mind was whirling, and I staggered a step when I stood. *Of course!* The big blingy red embellishments in Ava's kit. The crystals in Dianne's booth. Where better to hide gems than in plain sight, especially in a booth that was tucked out of the way behind a giant macrame screen?

Unless, of course, somebody like Ava came along and bought them before you could retrieve them.

My stomach roiled. *This* was the connection between the murders. It had to be. When the thief couldn't find the jewels at Ava's, he must have believed that Dianne still had them in her stock.

"But how would he know that Ava had them?" I murmured. The only way was if he—or she—*witnessed* Ava buying them or... I staggered backward, barely balancing on my heels and somehow managed not to twist my ankle. *Or if he was in my class and heard Ava griping about leaving them at home.*

Nikki cocked her head like an inquisitive sparrow and cupped my elbow to help steady me. "Did you say something, Tash?"

I pressed a hand to my stomach, which was threatening to empty all over Graciela's back room. "You say they caught the thieves?"

"They made an arrest around dinner time today, yeah, but—"

"I've got to go." I set the papers on a shelf—I could come back and straighten them later—and took Nikki by the hand. "Come on, honey." I glanced at her bag. "Unless there's something else in there you need to put back?"

She flushed and looked down. *Uh-oh. Guilt reaction.* "No."

"You're sure? I'm not going to judge you."

She shook back her hair and met my gaze. "I'm sure. And if you get me that recommendation, I'll see a counselor, Tash, I promise."

"That's all I ask. Now why don't you go on out and join the other ladies. I'm sure Evy could use a little support." I squeezed her hand and let it go.

"As long as it's not Virginia," she muttered, but she shouldered her bag and marched out onto the sales floor.

I hustled over to the receiving counter to dig through my purse. *I know I had Bae's and Huber's cards in here somewhere.* Normally I keep business cards in an antique silver cigarette case, but I'd been a little distracted lately, what with my friends getting murdered and my best friend being arrested.

The thief had to have been on the same MAX train as PJ on Saturday. He could have picked up the feathers at the Expo Center after PJ bought the boa. Well, he wouldn't have had to pick them up—they'd have stuck to him like burrs. He could have seen PJ at my class— I froze with my Fenty lip gloss in my hand. *Hold on a minute.*

There hadn't been any men *in* my class.

I huffed an impatient breath. Men came into the store all the time. Granted, the clientele was weighted heavily toward women, but there were enough male customers that one wouldn't have raised a red flag. PJ had made so many trips back and forth to Ava's car that day that he'd have made a perfect scapegoat if the thief had been lurking then. In fact…

The guy in the black hoodie. PJ had complained about him at the time—*and* had mentioned him peeling out of the parking lot after Ava.

"Aha!" I pulled Bae's card out of the inside pocket. As much as I wanted to spring PJ from jail as soon as possible, I needed proof of the connection.

And for that, I needed Ava's kit.

I hadn't seen it in PJ's apartment when I'd fed Mary Pickford —not that it was easy to see with all the sneezing—but PJ was a systems engineer and his apartment was even more organized than my craft room. Anything that didn't have a permanent home with him was parked on a table inside his door, and it had been empty.

Moocher.

I crumpled Bae's card in my fist. Good lord, the kit must still be in the back of PJ's car. When the police showed up to arrest him, the proof of his innocence was *right there.*

Wait—would the detectives believe that the presence of the rubies was proof of PJ's innocence, or would they think it gave him a motive? *No, that's stupid.* For one thing, why would he need to kill anybody if he knew he had the jewels? Plus, PJ had been stuck on MAX with everybody else on Saturday when the theft was taking place. Surely MAX had surveillance cameras that would give him his alibi.

One way or another, I needed to turn the gems over to the police, so I pulled out my phone. The card listed both the department number and a personal line. I tried the personal line first, but it went to voicemail.

"Dang it!" I didn't really want to leave a long involved voicemail, but I also didn't want to go haring off to retrieve the contraband without letting the police in on the deal—that would be the perfect way to get myself added to the suspect list, especially since I'd been at all the crime scenes.

I tried Huber's direct line instead. Voicemail. Double dang it. Why did they give out their numbers if they weren't going to answer? I called the department number.

"Washington County Sheriff's Office. How may I direct your call?"

"Could I please speak to Detective Bae?"

"One moment." While I waited for the call to connect, I drummed my nails on the counter, probably harder than necessary, since it prompted a startled look from a customer passing the open doorway. "I'm sorry, but Detective Bae is unavailable right now."

Blast. "Detective Huber then?"

"I'm sorry, but both detectives are tied up at the moment. Would you like to leave a message?"

"No, but thank you." I hung up. If I was going to leave a message—and apparently that was my only option—I'd rather use their direct lines and cut out the possibility of the message going astray or sitting on their desks until the next time they were in the office.

I dialed Bae again. After the beep, I took a breath. "Detective, this is Tash Van Buren. I think I've discovered the connection between Ava's death and Dianne's, and it's related to that jewel theft at the Convention Center. I think I know where the jewels are, and I'm going there now to retrieve them. If you could meet me at the Parthenon Apartments on SW Erickson Avenue in Beaverton, unit C10, I think we can clear PJ and return the jewels to their owners. I should be there in about fifteen minutes, but if you can't make it by then, don't worry. I'll wait."

I left the same message on Huber's voicemail, then stuffed everything back in my purse. I'd organize it later. Right now, I had places to go and a best friend to spring from the hoosegow.

CHAPTER TWENTY-ONE

I'd reckoned without the scrapbooking circle. The instant I stepped out of the backroom, Virginia hustled over and grabbed my elbow to tow me behind the custom stationary display. She pressed a rose-shaped die into my hand so hard the edges pricked my palm.

I frowned at it. "Virginia, I really don't have time to answer Cuttlebug questions right now."

"It's not a question." Her gaze cut to the side. "It's the die I told you I wanted, and that Ava bought out from under me. She never used it. She just carried it around in her kit." Virginia swallowed hard. Her pale cheeks turned red and blotchy, clashing with her auburn curls. "So I took it three weeks ago." Her face twisted in disgust. "She never even noticed, that's how much it meant to her."

"Virginia, I really don't think—"

"But I didn't kill her. Even if I said I wanted to."

I tried to control my exasperated sigh, but judging by the sharp glance she cast me, I didn't succeed. "I know that. But I really can't—"

"Tash?" Evy's wavery voice preceded her as she peeked around the display. "Do you have a minute?"

I glanced at my watch. "Actually, Evy, I—"

"It'll only take a second. I promise."

Virginia backed away, palms up as if warding off any attempt I might make to return the die to her. "My conscience is clear now. Remember that."

Evy watched Virginia stalk over to the craft table to retrieve her kit. "What's up with Virginia? I didn't think she *had* a conscience."

I blinked at Evy. She'd sounded almost as tart as PJ, something that had never happened before. "It's nothing. She just wanted to, um, return something to me. Now I really have to go."

She gripped my arm. "Please, Tash. You're the only one who'll understand." She held up her hand, thumb and forefinger measuring a tiny distance. "No more than half a second."

I made myself smile at her. Evy might be the most hopelessly inept crafter I'd ever met, but she was endlessly optimistic, good-hearted, and enthusiastic. "Oh all right." I tried not to huff. *Another epic fail.*

She heaved a huge sigh and released my arm. "*Thank* you. Well, the thing is, last month... Or was it the month before? No, wait, it was before that, because we'd just had the St. Patrick's Day class where you helped me with those shamrock cards, remember?"

"Yes, but—"

"Those were so cute!" She beamed at me. "I hope you'll do the same class this year. Although the Easter egg cards were just as lovely. I still have one tacked to my cork board at home as inspiration. Maybe you could do a double class with both this year?"

"Evy, I appreciate the compliment, but if that's all you needed to talk about—"

She blinked. "Oh. Didn't I say?"

"Not yet." Luckily I could still smile with gritted teeth.

"The thing is, the week after that class... Or maybe it was the week before. Or—"

"Evy."

"Right. Anyway, Ava offered to embellish one of my scrapbook pages for me. The one about my family trip to New York where we saw that wonderful burlesque show. What was it called? Theatre... Theatre something with letters. XIV, yes, that was it. Their costumes were a-*maz*ing." She giggled a little unsteadily. "What there was of them, if you know what I mean. Then we went to a Broadway show but couldn't get into the one we wanted. But somehow we managed to get last-minute tickets to a different show that let out so late we had to eat at the all-night diner. Then my hubby got food poisoning from his undercooked eggs and he was mad that I actually scrapped a page that included a picture of him hugging our hotel room's toilet. Remember?"

"I do." Unfortunately.

"Well..." She bit her lip and glanced over her shoulder. "I told her no." She winced, as if expecting a blow or a reprimand.

"You told who no? And why?"

Her eyes widened as if she couldn't believe I hadn't followed. "Ava. She offered to help me with the pages and I said no."

"That's it? You just refused her help?"

She nodded. "I know it was ungrateful, and now that she's dead, I feel so bad. I mean, it wouldn't have hurt me to be kinder, and now it just seems so... so prophetic, you know?"

My eyebrows rose. "Prophetic? How?"

"Well, I mean the page was all about my husband's suffering after a wonderful day of fun. And then, only *three months later*, she's killed after you guys had a day of fun at the scrapbooking expo." Her brow knotted. "Unless it's four months."

I patted her shoulder. "Evy, I'm sure that Ava never gave your refusal a thought." *Because she'd probably gone on to bully Nikki or taunt Virginia.* "You don't need to feel bad."

"But if I had just accepted her help, she might be alive today!"

My hand froze mid-pat. Evy's logic was convoluted on the best of days, but this one? "I don't think Ava's death had anything to do with your scrapbook. But I really do have to go."

"Oh, but, Tash, there's something else."

"Later, Evy." I hurried out of the custom stationary corner, noticing that neither Virginia nor Nikki were still at the tables. As I reached for the door, Graciela looked up from ringing up a customer.

"One second, *mija*."

I shot her a harried smile. "I'll call you later, hon. But I have to leave *right now*."

I escaped out the door and raced to my car. If I pushed it a little, I could make it to PJ's only a few minutes later than I'd promised Bae and Huber, assuming they'd gotten my message at all. Technically, the time wouldn't really matter. After all, Nikki said they'd caught the thieves, so nobody would be looking for the jewels anymore. But I didn't want PJ to have to spend one more needless minute behind bars. I'd wait all night if I had to.

When I pulled into PJ's apartment complex, the street lamps near his unit were flickering, casting weird shadows and doing nothing to lessen the dark. I shook my head. Although the complex was in a nice part of Beaverton, it wasn't kept up as well as it should be. I wanted PJ to move, but he claimed he'd made his nest and he was going to perch in it until a man with appropriately handsome plumage offered him a better option.

My headlights swept across his covered parking spot, gleaming on Moocher's cobalt paint. There was no sign of Bae or Huber yet, so I parked in the visitor spot directly opposite and hurried across the asphalt to peer in Moocher's rear windows. I huffed out a sigh when I spotted the kit.

My fingers trembled a bit as I located Moocher's key on my ring, but I managed to unlock the rear doors. I pulled the right one open and leaned in to grab the kit. I hesitated, my hands on the straps. Should I wait for Bae and Huber? But what if the embellishments weren't still in the kit?

A chill chased through me. If the jar wasn't in the kit, it meant that PJ—or somebody—had taken it out. As much as I trusted PJ, this thing had been sitting here, in full view of anyone who wandered by since Sunday afternoon's class. I had to be sure.

I eased the zipper open and peered inside. A jumble of dies sat on top. As I picked them up to set them aside, I caught a flicker of movement out of the corner of my eye. *Bae and Huber must have arrived.*

But when I straightened up, it wasn't the detectives. A figure all in black, including a balaclava, was rushing toward me. In this uncertain light, and with my heart pounding in my ears, I couldn't judge the person's size or gender, but I recognized the long, shiny object they were brandishing over their head.

Golf club.

As I stood frozen, my hand clutching the edge of the door, all I could stupidly think was *"Fore."*

CHAPTER TWENTY-TWO

They were moving fast. Silent. Almost on me. My hand seemed paralyzed, Moocher's door cutting into my palm. As they raised the club, its shaft glinting in the uncertain light, I shook myself out of my stupor and thrust the door into their path, flinching backward so the club clanged on the top of the door. *That's gonna leave a dent.* But I knew PJ would forgive me—better Moocher's door than my skull.

I grabbed the end of the club, hung on for dear life, and yanked. This close, I could tell the person was smaller than me, but so many people were that it still didn't give me a good read on their gender. Regardless, they had one heck of a grip and didn't let go, although they slammed into Moocher's open door, their arm extended over the top. I still held the dies in my other hand, so I jabbed them into their hand once, twice, three times until they let go with a high-pitched shriek.

But I lost my grip too, and the club clattered to the cracked asphalt.

I had a whistle in my purse, but I couldn't dig for it now, so I stomped both feet on the club. Since I learned that people respond to fire faster than the word help, I shouted, "Fire! Please, somebody, help! *Fire!*" For good measure, I added a scream supported with every ounce of my breath. PJ claimed I could give foghorns a run for their money, but unfortunately with all my nerves on edge, my throat was drier than the Sahara Desert and I couldn't force out more than a squawk.

On the other side of Moocher's open barn door, the assailant was muttering, "Shut up. Shut up. Shut up." They were scrabbling for the other end of the club, so I crouched down and grabbed the business end. But they got hold of the handle at the same time, yanking it toward themself so my shoulder jammed into Moocher *hard*. I eased back enough to brace my foot against the door—*dang, these pink kitten heels will never be the same*—and wrenched the club toward myself. I was rewarded by a satisfying thud when they collided with Moocher again, although it jolted my leg all the way to my hip.

Yank. Thud. Jerk. Jam. We played that game for a minute until an extra-fierce jerk on their behalf made me hit my head on the door frame, my foot slipped out of my shoe, and I lost my grip. Between my ringing ears and my missing footwear, I had to brace my arms on Moocher's bumper to keep from falling, my body blocking the interior.

"Move," the person barked. Their voice, muffled by the balaclava, nevertheless held a note of desperation. I hoped it was because their hand was painful—in the flickering light, I could see blood glistening on it from the die cut. "I don't want to hurt you, but I will if I have to."

"Is that what you told Ava?" My own voice shook, my head still spinning from the blow. "Is that what you told Dianne?"

They made a sound like somebody had hit them in the stomach. *Oh, if only someone would.* "That had nothing— I didn't — Just *move*."

"No." Yeah, it was stupid, but in my defense, I'd just banged my head pretty hard, plus my best friend's freedom depended on keeping this evidence intact. "I won't."

"Then this is your own fault." As they lifted the club, I raised my arms in front of my face, closed my eyes, and crouched, preparing to launch myself into their stomach and hopefully under the major force of the blow.

Thunk.

The sound of the strike was unmistakable, but I didn't feel any pain. I cracked my eyes open in time to see the club fall from the person's hand. They crumpled to the ground, revealing —

"Nikki?" I lowered my arms, wondering if the blow to my head was making me hallucinate. "What in the world are you doing here?"

She was staring down at the unconscious attacker, holding a Cuttlebug like a baseball bat. "I wanted to talk to you about returning some bigger things that I might have, um, accidentally taken, and I heard you say you were coming over here."

I glanced down at the attacker who was stirring a little and groaning. "I guess you weren't the only one who overheard me." I needed to be more discreet when I made calls about murderous motives—not that I intended to be involved in something like this ever again. "I thought they'd caught the jewel thieves. You said they'd made an arrest."

"Yes, but only one of them. He had an accomplice, although the police didn't release any information about them." She lowered the Cuttlebug. "Do you suppose Graciela will want this back if it's been, um, used?"

I sank down to sit on the edge of Moocher's tonneau. "Oh, honey. If she doesn't, I'll buy it myself and mount it on my wall." I started to laugh. "PJ claims crafting is dangerous. But apparently the danger can cut both ways."

Headlights swept across us once, twice, followed by flashing red and blue lights. Nikki hugged the Cuttlebug to her chest. "Is that the police? Are they here to arrest me?"

I pushed the other door open and patted the carpet next to me, beckoning for her to join me on Moocher. "No, honey. They're here for another reason entirely." I nudged the attacker's twitching leg with the toe of the shoe I was still wearing. "But they'll be getting an unexpected bonus." I frowned at Bae and Huber as they stepped out of their dark sedan. "Although they could have arrived a little earlier and saved us both some trouble."

The detectives stopped on the other side of the prone attacker. "Ms. Van Buren," Bae said, his face set in its usual granite lines, "why did you ignore my call?"

I blinked at him. Dang, my head was really starting to hurt. "Call? What call?"

"After I got your message, I called you back and told you that *under no circumstances* were you to attempt to retrieve the jewels on your own, since the thief's accomplice was still at large."

I nudged the person's leg again. "Not anymore."

Huber made some kind of sound and turned away, her shoulders shaking. She beckoned to the deputies in the other car and asked them to call for the EMTs.

Bae shook his head, then knelt down next to the attacker and pulled off the balaclava.

Except it wasn't *their* balaclava. It was most definitely *hers*.

I gaped at the woman's face, rubbing my aching head. "Brittany? But... but you were in my class." The silent one, who hadn't started her card. I peered at her more closely as she scowled up at Bae. "And *she* was the one who barreled into me at the Expo Center. The one in the red hoodie. I *thought* she looked familiar."

Nikki tilted her head and studied the glowering woman. "She's been in Central Paper a lot, too. I've seen her a bunch of times." The detectives stared at her, unblinking, and she bit her lip. "What? I notice things, okay? She was there tonight. She was wearing a red hoodie then, too, not black."

"Which was how she knew where I was going." Yep. Definitely had to be more discreet about those calls.

Bae stared down at the woman. "You have the right to remain silent—"

"Oh my god, PJ would *kill* to hear somebody being Mirandaed." I winced. "That didn't come out right." And now that I thought of it, he'd probably been read his rights too, when they came to arrest him.

PJ.

As soon as Bae finished his spiel, I stood up, only wobbling a little, because, hey—still missing a shoe. "Detective, you have to call the jail immediately and get PJ released."

"In due time. Could you show us the alleged jewels?"

"Alleged nothing. I'm sure of it." I turned around a little too quickly and swayed on my feet.

"Tash," Huber said, "are you all right?"

"I'm fine. Just bumped my head during the fight."

"Fight?" Bae barked. "There was a fight?"

"Of course there was a fight," I said tartly. "You don't think she just laid down in the parking lot to wait for you because I asked her nicely, do you?" I pointed to the golf club. "She came at me with that."

"She hit you?" Bae's expression turned even more grim, which I didn't think was possible.

"No. She tried. But we had a little tug of war with the club and I banged my head pretty dang hard on Moocher's door."

Bae's eyebrows rose. "Moocher?"

"Moocher the MINI. PJ's car."

Huber chuckled. "Nice."

Bae shot her a dirty look. "Then did you hit her?"

"No." Nikki hesitantly raised her hand. "That was me. She was about to hit Tash, so I, um, bonked her with this." She handed the Cuttlebug to Bae.

He hefted it in his hands. "We'll need to impound this. And the two of you may need to testify at any upcoming trial."

Nikki glanced wildly at me. "You're arresting me? Because I —"

"Not your trial, miss." Huber patted Nikki's arm and jerked her chin at the woman on the ground. "Hers."

"Hers." I tapped my bare toes and crossed my arms, fixing her with the stare that set tardy vendors shaking in their boots. "Is your name even Brittany?"

She didn't answer, but Huber said, "No. It's Kathleen Berglund."

Dang it, Kathleen had nearly let my best friend take the fall for her crimes. Now I wished I *had* hit her. "You framed PJ with those feathers."

She glared up at me. "He sure scattered enough of them around. But it wasn't my idea. Al came up with it after he missed grabbing the stuff at the craft show and when you didn't have them at the class." She clapped her hand over her mouth. Sue me, but I confess I was pleased that a little blood still oozed from the cut. *I guess I did get to hit her after all.*

I blinked. "Wait. Was Al the guy who nearly knocked PJ on his keister in the Expo Center parking lot?"

She nodded, letting her hand fall away. "I didn't want to hurt anybody. I *didn't* hurt anybody. That was all on Al."

"Really?" Bae snapped on a nitrile glove and picked up the golf club. "It certainly looks like you intended to."

"That was just for show," Kathleen muttered. "I didn't think I'd have to *use* it."

An ambulance pulled into the complex and cut its siren. The uniformed deputies helped Kathleen to her feet, cuffed her, and led her toward the waiting EMTs. Just before they reached the ambulance, she looked over her shoulder and met my gaze. "I still think it was a really good class."

"Not good enough, apparently," I muttered as I dug in Ava's kit. "Not if it provoked homicidal rage in my students."

Huber chuckled again. "Only one of them. And if her claims prove out, the homicidal one was probably the man we already have in custody."

"Sarah." Bae's voice held a definite reprimand.

"*Cam.*" She matched his tone, but added an edge of mockery. She handed me my shoe. "I believe this is yours. And since you're not wearing cocktail gloves today, perhaps you could let us retrieve the evidence?"

I glanced down at the kit. *Shoot.* "Right. Sorry. I wasn't thinking."

"And while we do that," she said sternly, "you need to get checked out by the EMTs."

I shook my head. *Mistake.* "I'm fine."

She gave me an admonitory glare as she donned her own gloves. "Head injuries are nothing to trifle with. If only for my own peace of mind, humor me."

"Tash, please?" Nikki clutched my hand. "Don't take chances, okay?"

I sighed. I didn't want to waste any time getting PJ out of jail, but I wasn't stupid. Huber was right, and I knew it. Head injuries, even minor ones, should always be taken seriously. I nodded at the kit as I slipped on my shoe. "It's in there. A jar of red embellishments."

She cocked an eyebrow. "Embellishments?"

"Crystals. Gems. Buttons. Really shiny objects. When Ava left her kit behind on Sunday, it tipped over and the contents spilled out. PJ and I noticed that some of the bling was really, er, extra blingy. But it never occurred to us that the jewels might be real."

"No reason you should." Huber withdrew the jar carefully, holding it up in the uncertain light. "I imagine the thieves never intended for things to escalate so far." She pressed her lips together and shot me the look a mother might give a recalcitrant toddler. "But please consider your actions carefully should you ever be faced with something like this again. Don't put yourself in unnecessary danger. Criminals, as evidenced by their crimes, have already proven that they rate their own self-interest above anything or anybody else."

"Don't worry." I let Nikki take my arm, but I wasn't sure whether it was to help me walk to the ambulance or for her own comfort. "After this experience, I don't intend to come any closer to a murder than the nightly news for the rest of my life."

Other than a headache, I was already feeling better by the time the EMTs cleared me, prescribing rest and ibuprofen. The uniformed deputies followed the ambulance with Kathleen handcuffed to a stretcher inside, but Bae and Huber were still huddled around Ava's kit. Nikki stuck to my side like a burr as I walked over to them.

"Detectives, have you called the jail to tell them to release PJ yet?"

Huber eyed Bae, who turned away to poke at the bloody die on the ground. "Not yet."

"Well, do it!" I bit my lip. Maybe getting belligerent with the police wasn't the best way to get them to cooperate with me. "I mean, please. Don't make him spend a night in jail." I glared at Bae. "He shouldn't have ever been arrested in the first place."

Bae held up his hand, the die pinched between his thumb and forefinger. "Would you mind telling us about this?"

I crossed my arms. "Are you going to call the jail?"

He heaved a sigh. "The jail has protocols about when and how prisoners are to be released—"

"But he was wrongfully arrested! You have the real culprits."

Huber held up her hands in their blue gloves, palms out. "Don't worry, Tash. As soon as we've bagged the evidence, I'll make the call." She gave Bae the side-eye. "After all, we wouldn't want anyone questioning our motives or accusing us of inappropriate behavior, now, would we?" Bae ignored her. "But in the meantime, if you could answer Detective Bae's questions, we'll get done all the sooner."

Right. That made sense, I suppose. I walked them through the scene, pointing out the dent in poor Moocher's door. Bae's expression darkened as he studied it.

"If that blow had connected with you, she could have seriously injured you. If she came armed—"

"I think she was probably armed to break Moocher's window and grab the kit," I said slowly. "Otherwise she'd probably have picked a more effective weapon." *Like a Cuttlebug.*

But because of that dent, Bae called for the crime scene techs to come out, and they took *another* hour, although at least they didn't impound Moocher for evidence. PJ would have been heartbroken.

And then *finally* Huber called the jail and told them to begin the process of releasing PJ. And though I was determined to be there when he was freed, Huber wouldn't allow me to drive myself. Instead, she drove me in my SUV, with Nikki following in her Corolla and Bae bringing up the rear in his detectivemobile.

It was too bad PJ couldn't see it. He dearly loved a parade.

CHAPTER TWENTY-THREE

As soon as PJ walked through the door, free once more, I had to swallow a lump in my throat. He was in his normal work clothes again, not that nasty orange jumpsuit, but his button-down was wrinkled, the collar unbuttoned. His usual bow tie dangled out of his pants pocket. I hurried over to him and enveloped him in a hug. He tried to pull away.

"Eww. LaTashia. You don't want to touch me. I've got *jail* all over me."

"I don't care. I'm just so glad you're out."

He sighed and then wrapped his arms around me, hugging me back with enough force to make me *ooomph*. "So am I, darling. So am I. When they told me I was being released, I thought I'd be in there for another week at least. Don't the weighty wheels of justice creak along more slowly, greased as they are with paperwork in triplicate? "

I chuckled. "So many mixed metaphors in there, Peej. But I don't think Bae wanted you locked up overnight any more than I did."

We stood like that for a minute, then he let go and stepped back, turning away to brush irritably at his cheeks—as if I didn't know he was crying. I had to blot my own eyes as well, and since I'd unloaded my tissues on Evy, I had to use my beautiful but totally impractical lace-trimmed handkerchief.

Oh, well. It would recover. How many times would I have a chance to spring my bestie from the clink? *With luck, this will be the only time.* "Are you ready to go home?"

He looked at me as if I'd sprouted two additional heads. "Do you even need to *ask* that question?"

I chuckled and linked my arm with his. "Do you want to stop for pancakes on the way?"

He shuddered. "God, no. All I want to do is wash this place off my skin. If I could shampoo my brain, I'd do that, too." He peered up at me. "How did you know they were releasing me tonight?"

I huffed. "I insisted on it. Once they had the second jewel thief in custody—"

"Wait, wait, wait." He unhooked his arm and held up his hands in a *time-out* T. "When you say *the second jewel thief,* that brings up several questions. One—there's a first thief? And two —what jewels? Clearly I'm missing large portions of this particular plot line."

"Well, I didn't find out about the jewels until tonight either." I filled him in, his eyes growing wider and wider behind his glasses.

"Oh my god. That was a *real* ruby?" He clapped a hand to his forehead and tottered over to lean against the wall.

My eyes prickled again. If he hadn't lost his tendency to overdramatize, then his stay in the slammer hadn't broken his spirit. *He'll be okay.* "I have some bad news, though."

"Worse than how close we came to sticking an *actual freaking ruby* to a Christmas card? Worse than a couple of reprobates trying to pin *two freaking murders* on me?" He pointed both index fingers at his head. "Worse than the absolute *disaster* my hair is right now?"

I winced. "Maybe?"

He covered his eyes with one hand. "Tell me. Rip the Band-Aid off. Show no mercy. I'm accustomed to suffering by now."

"When the second thief came at me with the golf club—"

"What?" He dropped his hand and his attitude and grabbed my arms. "Somebody had the *audacity* to attack you with a *blunt instrument*?" He growled—he actually growled. "It's a good thing we're still at the jail, because I need to get reincarcerated so I can beat the snot out of anyone who would *dare*."

"I thought you didn't believe in violence?"

"Ordinarily, no. But there are some lines that simply cannot be crossed—and threatening harm to you, whether personal, professional, or even imaginary—is number one on that list."

I hugged him again. "I love you, too."

"Damn right, you do." He released me and straightened his suspenders. "And in case you were wondering, that was indeed worse news."

I bit my lip. "That, um, wasn't actually the news."

His jaw sagged. "There's *more*?"

"The golf club missed me." I screwed up my face, peering at him from squinted eyes. "But it didn't miss Moocher. I'm afraid there's a dent in the top of the right rear door."

For a moment, he just stared at me. Then his teeth clicked together, a muscle bunching in his cheek, and he marched toward the door back into the jail. "That does it. I'm turning myself in. Because if I wasn't a murderer before, I will be now."

I caught his arm. "Peej, it's okay. I'm sure the dent can be repaired."

He whirled and faced me, his eyes suspiciously bright. "To *hell* with the car. If that *jerk* swung his weapon with enough force to leave a dent..." His voice wobbled on the last word. "They could put Moocher through a compactor for all I care if it meant you'd be safe." This time, *he* hugged *me*. "Tash, he could have *killed* you."

"Actually, it was a she, so getting yourself locked up again wouldn't do you any good."

"So I'll do drag. She'll never see me coming."

I gripped his shoulders and held him at arm's distance. "Do drag if you want, but do me a favor and keep out of prison? I don't like being without my bestie."

He nodded sullenly. "Only for you. Although you're right. How many times have I said it? Orange is *not* my color." He straightened his shoulders. "Now, let's get the heck out of Dodge. I want to wash this whole experience out of my hair *tout de suite*."

Before we'd made it to the exit, my phone rang inside my purse with the *Cops* theme song ringtone I'd assigned to the detectives.

"Hold up. That's Bae or Huber. I should answer this in case they need to see us before we go."

PJ blinked. "Detective Hottie? I can't see him looking like this!"

"Calm down. It could be nothing." I pulled out the phone. "Hello?"

"Ms. Van Buren." I recognized the voice and mouthed *Bae* at PJ, who clutched his hair. "Are you still in the facility?"

"As a matter of fact, we are, although we were about to leave."

"Would you mind stopping by my desk first?"

"Yes, we could swing by." I ignored PJ shaking his head wildly. "Is there a problem?"

"Not at all. But Ava's daughter is here, and she'd like to speak with you."

My stomach sank. In my zeal to prove PJ's innocence, it had completely slipped my mind to call Rebecca and extend my condolences. "I see. We'll be right over." Bae gave me instructions on how to reach the detectives' bullpen and hung up.

"LaTashia Danielle Fredericka Van Buren, what are you *thinking*? I look like I've spent weeks in, oh, I don't know, *a jail cell*. I can't face him now!"

"It was actually less than a day, Peej."

He crossed his arms. "According to my fashion and personal hygiene monitor, it *felt* like weeks."

"Look on the bright side. At least you're not handcuffed this time."

"That's not exactly a comfort," he grumbled.

"I'm sorry, but Ava's daughter is with him. She wants to see me."

"Well, why didn't you say so?" He gestured toward the door. "Let's go."

We followed Bae's directions, but when I saw Rebecca slumped in the chair next to his cluttered desk, a tissue pressed to her eyes, my steps faltered. *Her locs are styled just like Ava's.*

PJ took my hand. "Don't worry. She's not going to blame you." He gnawed on his lower lip. "Although… Do you think she'll want Mary Pickford back?" His grip tightened. "Wait. Did you call the cat rescue league already?"

I grimaced. "Sorry. It slipped my mind." I straightened my spine. "If she wants her mother's cat, though, that'll be one less thing for both of us to deal with."

"Exactly," he said, although his tone wasn't as decisive as usual. *Well, he* has *been in jail for the fashion equivalent of weeks.*

Bae looked up and saw us. Something flickered across his face when he spotted PJ. I hoped it was guilt—he should have known PJ would never kill anyone. I glanced down at PJ, but he was studying the laminated instructions on how to change the coffee filters in the nearby kitchen nook. I decided not to mention PJ's ambition to infiltrate the women's prison in drag to the detectives.

We made our way over to the desk. "Rebecca?" I murmured.

She lowered the tissue and looked up at me. Her hair might be arranged like her mother's, but her chin was pointier and her eyes far less shrewd. "Are you Tash?"

"Yes. I'm so sorry for your loss." I freed my hand from PJ's and held out my arms in invitation. Rebecca stood up and stepped into my hug. PJ gave me a half smile and a nod—he always said my hugs were better than Prozac.

After a moment, she pulled away and dabbed her eyes with the tissue again. "Thank you. Not just for the sympathy, but for everything you did for Mama while she was alive. I know she wasn't the easiest person to get along with—"

"She was fine."

Rebecca shook her head with a wry smile. "You don't have to be polite. I grew up with her. I have no illusions. But from the way she spoke about you, I know she thought the world of you."

"Th-thanks." *She did?* I struggled to pick my jaw up off the floor. "Do you need any assistance getting things settled? I'd be happy to help, and I'm sure the other women in our scrapbooking group would too."

"That's kind of you, but I've engaged an estate sale agent to deal with most of Mama's effects before I sell the house." Her expression turned apologetic. "Although there *is* one thing you could do."

"Anything. Just name it."

She sighed. "All those craft supplies. Can I interest you in any of them—or maybe *all* of them?"

"Uh…" I glanced at PJ, but he was looking the other way, studiously avoiding Bae's stare. "Your mother's stock is considerable. I'm afraid I couldn't afford—"

"No, no!" She held up her hands, one of them still clutching a crumpled tissue. "You don't understand. I don't want anything for them. I want to *give* them to you. I'm sure it's what Mama would have wished."

"Well, in that case…" PJ, drat him, still wasn't looking at me. This was supposed to be his cue to talk me off the ledge of craft supply overload. "I'd be happy to accept. I'll get PJ"—I elbowed him in the ribs—"to help me box everything up."

PJ scowled at me, rubbing his ribs. "Mary Pickford," he whispered through clenched teeth.

"Oh! Right." I turned to Rebecca with an apologetic smile. "What about your mother's cat? Will you be taking her with you?"

She blinked. "Cat? She had a cat?"

"Yes," PJ said. "A fluffy little calico."

Rebecca shook her head. "She never mentioned a cat. We never had pets when I was a kid because I'm allergic." She shrugged. "Maybe the local cat rescue—"

"We'll take care of it." PJ patted her shoulder. "Don't worry about a thing."

After exchanging contact information with Rebecca and arranging a tentative time to meet her at the house over the weekend, PJ and I finally headed out of the building, vowing to never return.

PJ was still fussing about his hair and his rumpled clothes. "I have my standards. Now Detective Hottie thinks I look like a *sloven*. With limp hair."

I chuckled. "He wasn't looking at your hair when we left, Peej. He was looking at your butt."

PJ raised his eyebrows. "Really?" PJ peered under his own arm in an attempt to see his backside. "These pants always did make it look good, wrinkled or not." He grinned at me. "What do you know, LaTashia? Being suspected of assault with a deadly crafting whatnot might be the best thing to happen to my love life in years."

CHAPTER TWENTY-FOUR

Close to dinnertime the following Saturday, PJ shoved the last box of Ava's craft supplies on top of the veritable wall of boxes we'd stacked in his home office. We'd run out of room at my place halfway through the day, so he'd graciously—more or less —allowed me to store the last load in his apartment.

"Good lord, LaTashia." He wiped his forehead with the tail of his Browncoats T-shirt. "Between the stuff you already had and *this* mountain of crafting paraphernalia, you don't need Central Paper anymore. You can open your own store out of your apartment." He scowled at the towering stacks. "Well, out of your apartment and mine." He shot me a sly grin. "You know, if you'd ditch your SUV for a MINI like Moocher, you could have stowed all this at the front of your garage."

I snorted. "I'd rather buy a house than a MINI."

He tilted his head and looked up at me, tapping his lip with one finger. "You know, that's not a bad idea."

"Don't." I sat down in his Aeron chair. "You know that's on my personal bucket list. But there never seems to be any *time*."

"Then make time. Make time for *you* for a change." He levered himself up to sit on the desk. "Now that Ava, rest her soul wherever it landed, isn't around to demand the half of your free time that isn't occupied with *moi*, you'll have more than you can shake a stick at." He squinted at the ceiling. "Not that you're the type to shake sticks." He grinned, a little more wickedly. "That's *my* specialty."

I covered my eyes. "I don't want to know." As he chuckled, my nose started to tickle. "*Aaaashooo!*" I peeked out from under my hand—sure enough, Mary Pickford had sashayed into the room, teal feathers clinging to her whiskers. "Oh, shoot, Peej. I *still* haven't called the cat rescue league."

He rolled his eyes. "Just text me the contact info. Silly girl, you don't have to do *everything* yourself. But in the meantime..." He leaned across the desk and snagged a small plastic bottle. He shook it, its contents sounding like a maraca. "This is for you."

I rubbed my watering eyes. "What i- i- *aaashooo!* Is it?"

"Over-the-counter allergy meds, of course." He opened the bottle and tipped a tiny white pill into his hand. "Go on. Take it." He nudged a sealed bottle of water toward me. "Compliments of the management."

I accepted both of them and downed the pill. "Thanks, Peej. You didn't have to do that."

"Of course I did, my darling." He patted my shoulder. "I've *got* you and we've got each other. It's written in the stars."

A smile teased my lips. "In that case..."

"No." He reared back, holding his palms up as if to ward me off. "No no no. I recognize that smile. You've got *crafts* on the brain. Isn't it bad enough that I'll be *living* with a metric crap-ton of your infernal supplies for the foreseeable future?"

"Don't be like that. I'm helping my friend Margaret with a mosaic over at the tearoom, and we could really use your help." I wiggled the bottle, sloshing the last inch of water back and forth. "C'mon, Peej. It'll be fun."

He gave me the side-eye and scooped the cat up to cradle against his chest. "You have a very peculiar notion of *fun*, LaTashia."

"There'll be scoooones," I singsonged.

He averted his gaze, scratching the purring cat behind her ears. "I refuse to be drawn into your wicked schemes."

I grinned and took another sip of water. No matter how much he fussed ahead of time, he'd come around as usual. Because he was right, although maybe not in the way he meant. We *got* each other.

And always would.

What's Next?

A new Crafty Sleuth adventure is coming soon!

Mixed media and mixed messages…

When I take time off from my day job to help my friend Margaret with a mosaic at her steampunk-themed tearoom, I never expect to get embroiled in another murder investigation.

Make that *two* murder investigations. As my bestie PJ would say, "Are you *kidding* me?"

Worse, the investigations are hitting a little close to home: PJ's beloved cousin Del has, um, less-than-cordial relationships with both victims and is emerging as the prime suspect.

Although I have no trouble envisioning how to marry photographs, ribbons, and paints into a harmonious whole, I can't wrap my head around these conflicting facts and feelings. Could my instincts be *so* wrong? Could PJ's bearded cinnamon roll of a cousin *really* be a cold-blooded killer? The evidence says yes, but my intuition says no.

Why isn't distinguishing truth from lies as easy as separating buttons from beads? If I mention my suspicions to PJ, it could destroy our friendship. But if Del *is* guilty, PJ could be the next victim.

Uh uh. Nope. Over my dead body.

Although, at the rate things are going? Maybe that's a poor choice of words…

Mixed Media is the second in the Crafty Sleuth humorous cozy mysteries, featuring edge-of-forty, plus-sized African American mechanical engineer Tash Van Buren—aka the Craft Whisperer—and her best friend, PJ Purdy. Count on creative crafts, fabulous fashion, and brisk banter—embellished with a pinch of mild profanity and peril.

I walked through the gift shop at the front of the tearoom, smiling at the display of my Alice in Wonderland cards. Margaret was right—I needed to make a few more, although they usually sold better in the spring during the Mad Tea Party teas. As I flipped the deadbolt on the plate glass front door, I was already imagining the Halloween display: mixed media shadow boxes; skull, skeleton, and bat earrings; decorated Mardi Gras styled masks; black cat and pumpkin fascinators with black netting as a fun veil.

When I held the door wide, PJ didn't walk in. Instead, he peered at me, his eyes narrowing. "LaTashia Danielle Fredericka Van Buren, I know that look. You're thinking about *crafting*, aren't you?"

I gestured for him to come inside. "Of course I'm thinking about crafting. You're delivering the supplies for the mosaic project yourself."

"That's *not* what I mean, and you know it." He marched past me, the bucket of coins held out in front of him, well away from his knee-length army surplus overcoat and black skinny jeans. "That's the *new* craft look, not the *ongoing* craft look. You're plotting new devilry."

I laughed, but...*hmmm. Devilry.* Maybe a few steampunk demons would fit right in.

"And there you go again." He sighed dramatically—and far too heavily, because he started coughing. "*Ugh.* This cleaning solvent is the worst."

I frowned at the bucket. "You followed the instructions, didn't you? The extra rinse? And you wore the ventilation mask, goggles, and gloves I gave you?"

He sniffed, leading to another cough. "I may not have your talent and artistic eye, but I'm perfectly capable of following directions. Of course I did. But the rinse was almost worse than the solvent." He poked a finger in my direction. "I trust you're working in an adequately ventilated area."

"Weeellll…" I hedged.

"LaTashia," he said, his voice dropping in weary warning.

"Don't worry. There's an exhaust fan, and besides, we're done working for the day. The odor will have dissipated by tomorrow."

"In that case, I suppose I can relent. But really, Tash, I don't know what you'd do if you didn't have me to take care of you."

"I imagine I'd manage." I kissed his cheek. "But I'm very glad I don't need to."

"Exactly. If you—" Through the open curtains separating the gift shop from the tearoom, he caught sight of Hank carrying another laden tray. "Oooh! Tea!" He hurried across the shop, pausing in the doorway to look over his shoulder. "What are you waiting for?"

"Not a thing," I said with a chuckle. "Although if you don't want to ruin the fragrance of the tea, not to mention the taste of Margaret's ginger scones, I'd suggest you take the coins back to the restroom."

He glanced at the bucket. "Good point." He sailed through the door, blowing a kiss to Margaret and Hank on his way.

"Don't forget to turn on the exhaust fan and close the door," I called.

"Really, LaTashia, this is *me* we're talking about. I never forget anything." His brow wrinkled, his mouth screwed up in thought. "Which is extremely unfortunate, because no matter how I endeavor, I cannot forget those dreadful paisley jeans I made the mistake of buying in high school." He shook his head.

"Ah, well. It was my Prince and the Revolution phase. I regret nothing."

He set the bucket inside the restroom, flipped the exhaust fan switch with a flourish, then closed the door and executed a deep bow.

I laughed. "Come here, you goof."

He trotted toward me, his black and white Chucks that matched my own flashing in the hallway lights, and linked his elbow with mine.

To many, PJ and I made an odd pair. Me, a six-foot-and-a-hair plus-sized Black woman, and PJ, a bespectacled hipster white guy several inches shorter—although PJ never copped to *short, small,* or *average*: "I'm *medium,*" he was fond of saying. But we shared a similar love of fashion, flair, and fun, and had become besties almost since the first moment we'd met during our first days at our mutual employer. Although I could never entice him to delve into a crafting projects on his own, he was always there to support me in whatever way I needed. We had each other's backs, and always would.

We joined Hank and Margaret at the table.

"Margaret, my love," PJ sang, "you're looking radiant as usual." He dropped a kiss on her cheek. "And Hank." He held out his fist for Hank to bump. Then they tapped both elbows and pretended to throw salt over their left shoulder in the weird greeting they'd developed since the first time the four of us had attended the Steam Pirates of the Air and Sea Con together. "Boo-yah!" He shed his overcoat, then plopped down in a chair and inhaled the steam drifting up from the teapot in front of him. "Mmmm. Is that what I think it is?"

Hank chuckled. "Of course. Malachi McCormick's Decent Tea. By now, I know better than to serve you anything else."

PJ held his hand over his heart. "You make me sound *inflexible*, my brother."

Hank reached for the teapot. "So you're willing to try a London Fog or a cinnamon plum tea?"

PJ slapped Hank's hand. "Paws off my Malachi. As if I'd ever betray him for bergamot or chamomile."

Hank smirked at him. "That's what I thought."

"Please," PJ said as he poured tea into a china teacup decorated with fluffy pink peonies, "I'm simply very faithful to those I love." He raised the cup to his lips and took a sip. "Mmmm. And I'm absolutely devoted to my Malachi."

Margaret leaned forward, squinting at what looked like a black smudge on the shoulder of PJ's Bad Robot T-shirt. "There's something on your shoulder, PJ."

He glanced down and his cheeks bloomed pink above his brown hipster scruff. "Drat. I thought I'd gotten it all. I really must find a better quality lint roller."

"It doesn't look like lint," Margaret said. "It looks like—"

"Cat fur?" I fluttered my eyelashes at PJ when he glared at me. "You might as well admit it, Peej. It's not like you're confessing to being an ax murderer." I winced. "Sorry." Although PJ's arrest for murder hadn't been ax-related, it definitely involved sharp implements, and he was still a bit skittish about it.

But today he waved it away. "Think nothing of it, LaTashia." He took another sip of tea and set the cup down on its saucer with a clink. "It's true. I'm fostering a cat." He made it sound like a combination of refined modern torture and Mother Teresa-level altruism.

"That's hardly a crime," Hank said.

"Not a crime, precisely." PJ bit into a scone morosely—which was quite a feat, as it was nearly impossible to consume Margaret's baking with anything other than complete bliss. "But it's such a cliche. A single gay man—a single gay *engineer*—with a cat." He popped another morsel of scone into his mouth. "But as I'm only *fostering* Mary Pickford, I shall recover presently."

"You named your cat Mary?" Margaret asked with a blink of disbelief.

"She's not *my* cat. She's a foster cat. And her name isn't *Mary*. It's Mary *Pickford*." He polished off the scone and reached for another. "Even though she's not present, we must show proper respect."

A Message from
Nelle & C.K.

Dear Reader,

Thank you so much for reading *Die Cut*, our first Crafty Sleuth cozy mystery. We hope you'll continue to follow Tash and PJ's further adventures in *Mixed Media*.

If you have time, we'd be so grateful if you could leave a review on Amazon, Goodreads, or other review sites. Reviews and word-of-mouth are more important than you can imagine to independent authors like us.

Active on Facebook? Then we'd love for you to join us in our Crafty Sleuth reader group!

All our best,
—Nelle & C.K.

Also by
Nelle Heran

With C.K. Eastland

Crafty Sleuth Mysteries
Die Cut
Mixed Media
Found Objects (coming soon)

Writing as E.J. Russell

Find E.J. on Audible at https://ejr.pub/ejr-audible

M/M Paranormal Romance and Mysteries
Mythmatched Universe
Quest Investigations Mysteries (Five Dead Herrings, The
Hound of the Burgervilles, The Lady Under the Lake, Death on
Denial)
Fae Out of Water Trilogy (Cutie and the Beast, The Druid Next
Door, Bad Boy's Bard)
Supernatural Selection Trilogy (Single White Incubus, Vampire
With Benefits, Demon on the Down-Low)
Other Mythmatched Romances (Howling on Hold, Witch Under
Wraps)
Possession in Session (free with newsletter signup)
Cursed is the Worst (free with YBBB promotion in 2022)

Enchanted Occasions (Best Beast, Nudging Fate, Devouring Flame)

Royal Powers (Duking It Out, Duke the Hall, King's Ex)

Other Stand-Alone (Purgatory Playhouse, Monster Till Midnight)

M/M Supernatural Suspense
Art Medium (The Artist's Touch, Tested in Fire, Omnibus edition)
Legend Tripping (Stumptown Spirits, Wolf's Clothing)

M/M Historical Romance (Silent Sin)

M/M Contemporary Romance (The Thomas Flair, Mystic Man, Clickbait, For a Good Time, Call…)

M/M Contemporary Holiday Shorts (The Probability of Mistletoe, An Everyday Hero, A Swants Soiree, Christmas Kisses)

M/F Contemporary Romance The Boyfriend Algorithm

Also by
C.K. Eastland

With Nelle Heran

Crafty Sleuth Mysteries
Die Cut
Mixed Media
Found Objects (coming soon)

Writing as C. Morgan Kennedy

Haven, Oregon Series
A Coffee-Driven Life (coming soon)
A Forgotten Life (coming soon)

.

About The
Authors

Nelle Heran (she/her) has always loved mysteries. She cut her teeth on Nancy Drew before graduating to Agatha Christie, Dorothy L. Sayers, Josephine Tey, and Charlotte MacLeod. Full disclosure: She stopped watching *Murder, She Wrote* when she began identifying the murderer before the opening credits finished rolling.

Nelle also writes LGBTQ romance and mystery as E.J. Russell (https://ejrussell.com). She lives in rural Oregon with her Curmudgeonly Husband, enjoys visits from her wonderful adult children, and indulges in good books, red wine, and the occasional hyperbole.

Find out more about Nelle, including social media links, at her website, https://nelleheran.com.

C.K. Eastland (she/her) fell in love with mysteries when she first discovered reruns of the original Hanna-Barbera series *Scooby-Doo, Where Are You?* Over time, she graduated to Sherlock Holmes and is currently addicted to *Midsomer Murders*.

C.K. also writes contemporary swirl romance mysteries as C. Morgan Kennedy (https://cmorgankennedy.com). Recently she moved from Portland, Oregon, to Chicagoland for her day job.

Still nesting in her new condo, C.K. spends her mornings and weekends researching famous Victorian homes, scrapbooking, and watching way too many Star Wars fandom reviews on YouTube.

Find out more about C.K., including social media links, at her website, https://ckeastland.com.

Acknowledgements

We owe a debt to so many for help and support on this book! Massive thanks go out to our fabulous editors, Shéa MacLeod and Meg DesCamp; to Markayla Blake of Covers in Color for giving us the covers of our dreams; to our wonderful beta readers—lyric apted, Lisa Leoni-Kinley, and Ann Turner; to Debbie, owner of Main Street Stamp and Stationary in downtown Tigard, OR, for giving us an all-access pass to her business (and for not laughing too loud—or calling the police—as we toured the store, exclaiming, "Oooh! You could kill somebody with this!"); to Maggie, owner of The Clockwork Rose Tea Emporium in downtown Beaverton, OR, and her husband Harold, who gave us a welcoming place to sip tea and laugh till our sides hurt. Support your local businesses!

From C.K.:
Crazy love and thanks to my personal cheerleaders Jessie Smith, Linda Mercury and her Charming Man, and the Retreat Beach Babes (my scrapbooking circle): Jen, Jan, Donna Lyn, Kim, Karen, and Anne. Nelle—you are an amazing partner in fictional crime.

From Nelle:
Love and appreciation to C.K. for being the inspiration for the Crafty Sleuth series (because she basically *is* Tash), and to my family—Jim, Hana, Nick, Ross, and Billy—for endless support.

And of course, from both of us, thanks to you, our readers, for accompanying us on this journey! Because of you, we can continue to do what we love!

Made in the USA
Monee, IL
01 July 2022

98732065R10121